Tails of Elbana

CATALYST
Book 1

By Lucy & Lizzy Grimm
Illustrations by Maggie Robinson

www.grimmsimaginarium.com

Second Edition

10 9 8 7 6 5 4 3 2

ISBN-13: 978-1979608428
ISBN-10: 1979608423

Dedication:

To our friends and family, thanks for your support. Thank you, Noriko, for reading and enjoying our story. Aunt Marie, the long wait for the first book in our dragon series is finally over. Thanks to Maggie for her brilliant artwork.

Maggie Robinson provided some fantastic artwork for us including: Cover Illustration Line Art for Meeka & Nata, Catalyst Title Font, and Interior Illustrations.

Lizzy Grimm did the design and painting of the Cover Art, the Series Logo, and importing and touching up all of Maggie's fabulous artwork.

Not to be outdone, Lucy Grimm designed and drew the map.

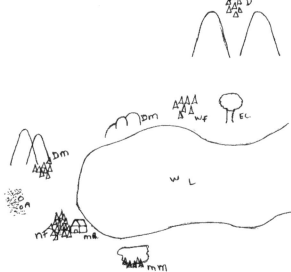

D - Orakonare
EC - elbano Colony
WF - Windle Forest
Dm - Drall mound
D m - Dark Mountain
o A - Oasis
n F - narlley Forest
mP - mAster Pukas
mm - mere maish

—Chapter 1—

Wind. Wind whipped through her hair, and whistled in her pointed ears. Riding on the back of Meeka, the sand dragon that lived with her family, was a thrilling experience. Nata enjoyed it as often as she could. In the distance, the grey mountains were ringed with puffs of white clouds.

"Faster Meeka!"

Meeka snorted. "Really Nata, if I fly any faster, you will undoubtedly fall off. Still, I do love flying fast. When the hunters get back, I will have to challenge Mooto to a race."

Nata giggled. "Only if Nole and I get to join

1

in."

"Deal."

Nata threw up her hands as the wind blew through her green hair. A blur of greens from the forest and grasses below flew past them. Flowers in bloom gave up their aroma to tease her nose. Nata patted Meeka's smooth purple scales.

Today, they were flying to Master Pukas's house. Master Pukas was a sorcerer who lived beside Narley Forest. Nata had never met him, but her papa had told her stories about him.

Her thoughts sobered. Her papa usually rode on Meeka, while he was looking for the roots, herbs, graf leaves, and cricket berries all over their world of Aquatia that he used to make medicines and poultices. Unfortunately, Mama was ill, and Papa had run out of the ammera flower that he needed to make her medicine.

Ammera flowers have thin red outer petals, and pointed yellow inner petals surrounding a blue-green center. The stem was thick with dark green forked leaves growing out of it. Aside from the flower's looks, the most important thing for her to remember was that the flower had a pungent scent that required a special pouch her papa had made to carry it in, otherwise the smell of the flower would make both her and Meeka too ill to carry it.

"How much farther is it to Master Pukas's house?"

Meeka dipped her head. "We are just about to

Whyttle Lake. Master Pukas's house is on the other side of it."

Luck was with them. They had been flying for several hours, but hadn't encountered any mountain dragons. If their luck held throughout the day, they shouldn't have to worry about being hunted at night as mountain dragons don't tend to be nocturnal. That didn't stop flying at night from having its own set of difficulties.

Nata looked down. Their shadows danced across the surface of the lake beneath them. She noticed a thin shadow floating ahead of them, and glanced up. Beside the lake sat a log house with white smoke drifting out of the chimney. A larger log building sat beside it with a wooden fence between them.

As Meeka flew lower, Nata was able to make out more details. Inside the fence, there was a beautiful blue horse with a black mane grazing on the grass. In front of the house, was a well with a bucket on the handle. What caught her attention the most was the dark green forest that seemed to loom behind the house, and made her feel a shiver of dread run down her spine.

"Is that Master Pukas's house?"

"Yes, hang on."

A rush of wind danced across her face, and sang in her ears from powerful wings braking their flight as Meeka landed with ease on the grass beside

Whyttle Lake.

"Nata, remember what your papa said. Don't disturb Master Pukas for a prolonged period of time. Just politely ask him for an ammera flower."

She sighed. "Yes Meeka."

Nata slipped from the saddle to the ground, then ran a cone comb through her green hair. She brushed off her leather riding pants, straightened her purple top, and smoothed out the green fur of her tail in an effort to make herself presentable. Being eleven, she was a little nervous and excited at meeting Master Pukas.

Feeling that she was as presentable as she could make herself, she turned her gaze back towards the house, and took a deep breath as she started to walk up to Master Pukas's house. It puzzled her that the house was on the ground, because, to her knowledge, all elbee homes were built up in the trees. As she got closer to the house, she could see that, despite the house being on the ground, it looked like it was built large enough to accommodate a sand dragon. That didn't mean that the house was huge. The torso of a sand dragon is comparable in size to the torso of a horse after all. When she reached the front door, she brushed off her riding pants again, swallowed, and gently knocked on the door.

Silence was all that greeted her.

Maybe Master Pukas was not—

Crash!

Bang.

"HERE!"

"HERE STOP THAT!"

Thud.

The sudden silence in the wake of all that noise made the fur on her tail puff out. She glanced at Meeka, who was busy drinking from the lake like nothing had happened.

Nata frowned.

Hmm... go inside or wait outside?

What if Master Pukas was hurt?

She knocked again. After getting no answer, Nata decided to go inside. Taking a deep breath, she opened the door, and tiptoed into the house.

"Master Pukas... are you here?"

A dust cloud hung in the air. Two big candles on the table glowed, and a pot of something was bubbling over the fireplace. Her earlier assumption about having room for a sand dragon inside the house appeared to be accurate, since there was a large enough open space inside to accommodate one. The table in the center of the room was cluttered with glass tubes, labeled bottles of all shapes and sizes, and stacks of books. Nata had never seen so many books in one place before. The walls were lined with bookshelves filled with lots of books. Her papa had a few books on medicines, but most knowledge in the Elbano Colony was passed down through the oral storyteller.

Despite her awe of so many books being in one place, what caught her attention the most was the cobwebs. Cobwebs everywhere. Hanging from the ceiling, the table, virtually every surface in the room had some sort of cobweb attached to it somehow. How there were cobwebs on everything when the room was clearly used escaped her.

"Achoo..."

The dust was atrocious. Her eyes blinked rapidly as she swiped her sleeve across them to stop her eyes from watering. A second glance around revealed a layer of mud and grime throughout the house. Honestly, the whole place looked like it could use a good cleaning.

"Ma—"

Snort.

Nata jumped.

She looked over into the corner to see two beady grey eyes peering at her. Given that there was only one occupant of the house, she could only assume the eyes belonged to Master Pukas, who was on the floor in a heap with books on top and all around him.

He was dressed in green shirt and pants with a rope belt tied around his waist. His mouth was framed by a short white goatee, while his white hair was braided into a round cap on his head. A green beret with a beautiful feather in multiple hues of green rested on the floor beside him. His legs and tail were all tangled up in what appeared to be a rope.

Nata felt her mouth twitch.

Hehe—mph.

She covered her mouth with her hand as she felt a giggle coming up. At the moment, she was rather thankful for the dust, since laughing in the old sorcerer's face was probably not the best way to introduce herself. She wheezed a few times before she got her breath under control, but just as she was about to speak again she was interrupted.

"Humph! So you are the one who banged on my door, interrupted my concentration, and caused my spell to go awry."

Nata paled. "Oh! Sorry Master Pukas. You see—"

"If you are going to barge in on a person, then the least you can do is help clean up the mess!"

Nata gulped.

Oh dear... not a good first impression at all.

He was busy untangling his legs from the rope, so she went over to start picking up the books around him. "Mind you, when you stack the books up, the bigger ones go on the bottom, and so forth."

"Yes Master Pukas."

Nata tried not to look at Master Pukas, who

was still struggling with the rope. She tried. Really she did, but it was like the rope had a mind of its own. It kept tangling around the sorcerer's legs, which caused him to dance around the room. She was having a hard time concentrating on stacking the books. Nata put her hand on her mouth to smother another giggle.

—Chapter 2—

The sorcerer's grey eyes were popping, and some of his hair came loose from the braids. What was even more astonishing was the fact that the loose hairs started braiding themselves again. That would have been fine, if not for the fact that the more frazzled he became, the more erratic the braids turn out to be. In no time at all, his braids were a massive tangle standing up from his head going this way and that. Finally, Master Pukas mumbled a few words, waved his hand in the air, and a blue flash appeared. Without further ado, the rope went slack as it fell to the floor.

"That will teach you," he addressed the rope as he picked it up off of the floor. "Now, why are you here?"

Nata bit her lip, and tried desperately not to look at the sorcerer's hair. "I'm Nata, daughter of Nomo, the Elbano Colony healer. My mama was poisoned by a nally bush. Papa sent me to gather an ammera flower for a medicine."

Master Pukas ambled over to the fireplace. "Hmmm..."

The pot was boiling over. Stew bubbled down the sides, popping and hissing as it went. She watched as he lifted the pot off the fire.

He frowned. "I see. Nami is ill, eh? Nomo has to realize how dangerous it was for you to come here on your own even with a dragon to protect you. Weren't there any warriors who could be spared from the colony?"

"No Master Pukas, the warriors are out hunting. Papa would have come, but he was afraid to leave Mama."

He stroked his goatee, while his hair untangled itself from the massive mess it had turn into, and began reweaving itself into the same braided cap he had when she came in.

How does his hair DO that?

On second thought, WHY does it do that?

While she was watching his hair with a clandestine eye, Nata finished organizing all of the books into stacks. The last thing that seemed out of place in the house was Master Pukas's hat. She shook out the dust as she picked it up, and put it on the table.

Why does he even have a hat?

With nothing else to do, she set about looking around the room again. Her gaze fell on a book sitting in a peculiar four sided book stand on the table, which had a cover made from brown deerskin. Etched on the book was a dragon with the most spectacular purple glowing eyes she had ever seen. Driven by curiosity as well as the fact that purple was her favorite color, Nata brushed her fingers across the coarse leather of the ancient book. Tingles ran through her fingertips, and transformed into tremors that raced up her arm.

What—

The book was jerked out from under her fingertips as the sorcerer spun the book stand to face him. "Don't touch that book."

"Sorry, M—M—Master Pukas."

The book stand on the table spins. Spins! That must be handy with so many books.

His gaze was stern as he assessed her sincerity. Apparently finding no lie in her demeanor, he swiped the book off the stand. Every movement he made screamed agitation to her as he turned his back, save for his tail which seemed to droop. With a surreptitious movement, she rubbed her hand to sooth the tremors, while he headed over to the corner. He placed the book on a separate book stand near the other books along the wall.

The stand was exquisite in design. It looked like someone had carved the wood in the likeness of a tree with roots for the feet of the stand, and branches woven together in order to make up the actual place for the book to sit. The stand stood about three feet high to where the book sat. She should know as the bottom of the book would reach the top of her head. If she had to guess, based on how tall he was in relation to the book stand, she would say that Master Pukas was somewhere around four feet tall. Of course, that would not be a surprise, since four feet is pretty normal for an elbee.

Nata swallowed as he turned, and headed back towards the pot of stew on the fire. She shifted from one foot to the other as she wrung her hands.

Isn't he going to say anything about the ammera flower?

Once he reached the pot of stew, it didn't take him long to gather table settings for two people. He ladled out the stew into the bowls that he placed on the table to join the cider he had poured into iron mugs from the jug that sat on the table. A jug that, miracle of miracles, had no cobwebs or dust on it at all. He nodded to her as he sat down in a big wooden chair at the table. She took that as her cue, and sat on the chair adjacent to him, while the last chair at the opposite end of the table remained empty.

"I don't have any ammera flowers at the moment. I used the last one up just last week. I was intending to go resupply my stock next week, but it looks like I'll have to make that a higher priority. For now, let's eat."

She slumped down in her chair in relief. "Thank you Master Pukas."

Nata picked up the bowl of stew, and started to eat. It tasted like burnt corn and charred wood. She choked, and guzzled some cider to wash it down. Apparently, her tail had picked up a lot of dust in its fur while she was helping tidy up, because a humongous cloud of dust came off of it when she lashed her tail in distress.

Master Pukas glanced at her, his bushy brows coming together over his wrinkled face. Nata winced. She gobbled the rest of the stew, and washed it down with cider as quick as she could. Then she sat in silence, waiting while Master Pukas stroked his goatee in deep thought.

While she was waiting, her gaze kept darting to the book with the etched dragon on it.

What kind of dragon is that?

It doesn't look like a mountain dragon, or a sand dragon.

Nata rubbed her hands together as she turned her eyes away from the book, and back towards her host. "Master Pukas, what about my mama?"

"I'm sure Nomo is not expecting you home today. I cannot give you an ammera flower that I do not have. Spree will be back from hunting in three days. We would have to wait until then. Or—"

Nata felt all the blood drain from her face.

Three days!?

He turned his back to her, but she could still hear the sorcerer muttering to himself. Her breathe was caught in her throat as she strained to listen for anything that might help her find the flowers faster. "... west, ... Narley Forest, ... flowers... base of the Dark Mountains."

That was all she needed to hear. With a last glance to make sure he wasn't paying attention to her, she tiptoed out of the house, and raced towards Meeka.

Meeka opened her eyes as she heard Nata come closer. "Nata what—"

"No time," she puffed. "Master Pukas doesn't have any of the flowers, and he wants us to wait three days in order to even go find them."

Meeka lashed her tail. "Three days?"

Nata wrung her hands. "Mama might not last that long. I did hear him say that the flowers grow west at the base of the Dark Mountains. We know what they look like, and that they smell terrible. It shouldn't be too hard to find them, if we try."

Meeka stretched out her spine and wings. "Base of the Dark Mountains... hmm..., and Dragon Mountain is just the other side. Clawing with mountain dragons no doubt."

"Please Meeka, can we go look for an ammera flower."

Nata's gaze darted back towards the house, worried that Master Pukas would realize she was missing and come after her, before some strange movement in the darkness of Narley Forest caught her eye. She shuddered. It almost felt like the forest had eyes.

"It'll be dangerous, but you're right. Your mama's health is not in good shape at all." Meeka nodded. "Alright let's go for it."

Meeka dipped her head down, Nata grabbed one of her smooth dark purple horns, and lifted herself up into the saddle. Just in time too, for Master Pukas came barreling out of his house. With a powerful beat of her wings, Meeka tore off into the sky leaving Master Pukas far below. She could hear him shouting for them to come back, but they couldn't wait three days. They just couldn't.

I hope our earlier luck holds out.

—Chapter 3—

*N*ata looked down at Narley Forest as they flew over it, but they were flying so high that it just looked like a dark blur. The distant mountains looked blue against the afternoon light of the suns, topped with a blanket of snow. Nata inhaled, and wrinkled her nose. Odors of decay drifted up from the woods below. Thoughts whirled around in her head like the eddies in the current of a river.

Why did his hair move all over the place by itself? What was with that book? Why did Master Pukas say we had to wait three days? The two of us could have flown on Meeka to get the ammera flower. I mean it's not like elbees are that heavy in comparison to a sand dragon... I only hope that we will find the ammera flowers without any mishaps... like mountain dragons, or whatever else may be in these lands.

They flew along in a companionable silence, so Meeka could listen and look for possible danger. A knot began to form in the pit of her stomach. There was no way for them to get the flower, and return home today. As such, they were going to have to return to Master Pukas's house for the night. She hoped that Master Pukas was not too angry with them.

I hope mama is going to be all right.

If we do stay at Master Pukas's, I hope he will let me fix something to eat.

Just the thought of eating more of that awful stew made her stomach lurch. She pressed a hand to her stomach just as Meeka let out an explosive sneeze.

"Meeka, what's wrong?"

"I believe I've found the ammera flowers. I can smell their pungent odor from way up here. Hold on, I'm going to land just this side of the forest."

Meeka circled once, and then landed in a patch of daisies, no more than a wingspan from a patch of ammera flowers. Daisy are one of the few flowers a sand dragon doesn't mind smelling. The swath of trees close by would provide some cover if they needed it.

Meeka sneezed. "There they are. Hurry and get one. The smell is terrible, and this place makes my scales itch."

Nata wrinkled her nose. "Okay, I'll be as quick as I can."

She scampered out of the saddle on Meeka's back, and darted over to the closest ammera flower. It was the biggest flower she had ever seen, as well as the thickest stem. Now she understood why she would only need to bring back one flower, because of the size.

I hope I can fit the flower into the special pouch my papa made.

Nata took out her small knife, and tried to cut the stem. It didn't work. The stem was so tough that the small knife would not even put a dent in it. In desperation, she tore at the stem with her claws.

Oh no! I wonder if Master Pukas had some sort of special tool to cut the flower stem.

Meeka gasped and sneezed. "Nata, what's taking you so long? Speak up."

She looked at Meeka, while her green eyes filled with tears of frustration. "Meeka, I can't get the knife, or my claws to cut through the stem. Can you use your claws to cut it?"

Meeka sniffed. "You want me to come over to that dreadful flower, and use my claws to cut it!?"

"Please Meeka!"

The afternoon was getting very hot by now, which added to her growing frustration.

"Oh very well..., but hold the flower away from me. I do not want its appalling smell in my face."

The flower did have an atrocious odor, and she was starting to feel a bit lightheaded. Nata held the stem so tight that when Meeka cut through it, she tumbled backwards. Lucky for her, because Meeka gave an explosive sneeze at the same time, burning a black spot in the ground where the flower had been standing. A flock of black crows tore out of the trees with cries that shattered the stillness.

Meeka whirled her head around, buried her claws in the ground to brace herself, and stared into the forest. Nata lay on the ground for a minute to catch her breath before she scrambled to her feet. She was relieved to see that the patch of green fur on her tail had not been singed off. Nata walked over to stand beside Meeka, so she could peer into the forest.

"Quick, put the flower into your pouch. It's time to get out of here."

Nata nodded. "Thank you, Meeka."

The forest stayed dark and silent, which gave her an eerie feeling. Looking at her pouch, she realized that it was far too small for the flower. At least, it was too small if she didn't want to crush the flower. She bit her lip. Well, Papa usually crushed up the flower to make medicine anyway, so she hoped that the flower would still be okay. She did her best to not crush the flower more than necessary as she put it in the special pouch, and sealed it up.

With one last look around to make sure she hadn't missed anything, she grabbed onto one of Meeka's horns, and heaved herself into the saddle. She had just gotten settled, when a terrific roar was heard throughout the area. Meeka and Nata both froze. Without further prompting, Meeka dove towards the shelter of the trees. Nata could hear the snap and cracking of branches as Meeka hurried to get farther undercover. Once they were far enough inside, Meeka turned around, and settled in to wait. Neither of them made any sound as the heavy beat of large wings filled the air over Nata's rapid heartbeat. Every now and then the wing beats were punctuated by another savage roar.

Dragons have a fantastic sense of smell. Why haven't they found us?

Oh of course, the flowers are overpowering our scent.

Thank goodness.

The wing beats seemed to be growing further and further away while they waited. A magpie that had not flown away with Meeka's first sneeze, started hopping towards them.

"Shoo," Nata hissed.

The magpie was either curious, brave, or foolish as it hopped closer still before it perched on

Meeka's back.

Nata used her tail to swipe the bird off. "No hitchhikers."

Meeka sighed. "I'm telling you, sometimes we dragons get no respect."

Nata giggled, and she could feel the tension in Meeka's muscles start to ease up when it appeared nothing was coming after them. All of the sudden Meeka took a large breath, then another, and buried her nose in a bit of moss on the ground. Nata was horrified to realize that Meeka was trying not to sneeze. Despite Meeka's best efforts, it was a losing battle as another loud sneeze tore through the air.

The resulting silence that greeted them was unnerving. When nothing happened after several moments, Meeka began to climb one of the trees near her, so that she could poke her head above the tops of the trees to check their surroundings.

Before long, Meeka pulled her head back beneath the canopy of trees, and hopped back down to the ground. "Looks safe enough."

Nata breathed out a sigh of relief. "Good, let's get out of here."

Nothing may have happened so far, but Nata had a peculiar feeling that the forest was watching them. In fact, the fur on her tail was standing on end. Meeka was quick to extract them from the forest, but she let out another sneeze as she lifted them up into the air. Nata expected them to fly back over Narley Forest, returning by the route they had come. Instead, Meeka began to fly south.

The flight was quiet, save for Meeka's snuffling in an attempt not to sneeze again. Nata felt her muscles bunch up underneath her skin, because all of the sudden Meeka was bobbing her head back and forth as if she was looking for something.

Oh dear, what now?

Endless brown sand passed below them, dotted with dinga cacti and okasha trees. Occasional ripples weaved across the sand's smooth surface. Tracks left by a snake. Vague dark shapes circled in the distant skies, while a haunting silence hung in the air.

Nata shivered in spite of the heat. On the ground ahead, something shimmered in the sand. She hoped it was nothing dangerous, since Meeka was flying right towards it. As they got closer, Nata realized it was an oasis, which Meeka circled once before she landed.

"All this sneezing has made me thirsty. After I get a drink, we will fly to Master Pukas's house, so stay on my back."

Nata dug the claws on her hands into the soft leather of the saddle. "Okay."

With nothing better to do she examined her surroundings. The oasis was encircled by okasha trees. The water reflected the twin yellow suns opposite twin blue moons in the sky. A brown desert fox cautiously approached the water, and sniffed the air. Its long ears stood straight up, while it drank.

Probably doesn't want to be a dragon's dinner.

"Meeka, what did you see in the forest?"

Meeka lifted her head from the water. "Nothing..., but we made an awful lot of noise, what with me sneezing and all, so I decided it would be safer to go a different way back to Master Pukas's house."

A turkey vulture flew up out of the trees, startling Nata into letting go of the saddle. It circled the oasis a few times before it let out a low guttural hiss as it flew away. The desert fox froze as it heard the hiss, tucked its tail between its legs, and fled.

Nata shuddered before she asked Meeka something to distract herself. "How did you know there was an oasis here?"

Meeka snorted. "Really Nata, a dragon doesn't need to see water to smell it."

Nata twisted her tail around her wrist. "Oh... you know your fire nearly singed my tail, sometimes I wish I had your hard scale armor."

Meeka's whole body shook with laughter. "I think you would look absurd with dark purple scales down your back and a light purple scaled abdomen."

Nata giggled as she imagined purple scaled arms. "I suppose it would."

Meeka sneezed again. "Nasty flowers."

Nata took a drink from her water skin, and

ate a piece of bread with some dried fruit. Meeka shook her head and snuffled. With a flap of wings, they left the oasis.

They had been flying for a while when Nata spotted something. "Look Meeka, I see something on the ground that sparkles."

Meeka slowed down. "Where?"

"Look down to the right. It's in the middle of the large sand dune."

"Ah, I see it now. Hang on. I'll fly lower, and pass over top of it."

Nata jolted. She only meant to point it out in case it was trouble, not to get closer to it. "We've run into a lot of trouble already today. Don't you think we are pushing our luck?"

"Nonsense."

Nata sighed. She should have known. Meeka was always on the lookout for more treasures to add to her hoard. Nothing for it, but to go along for the ride now.

The lower Meeka got, the more whatever it was sparkled, but now it seemed to give off a purple light, which perked Nata's interest. Purple wasn't her favorite color for nothing after all.

"I think it will be safe for us to land, but let me circle twice just to make sure."

It didn't take Meeka long to determine it was safe. She landed with a swirl of sand, and Nata climbed out of the saddle.

"Don't take too long to look at it," Meeka admonished.

Nata flashed Meeka a smile even as her tail quivered in excitement. "Don't need to tell me twice."

She darted across the remaining distance to the as of yet unidentified object. When she reached it, she found that there were actually two objects instead of one. The objects appeared to be two smooth purple stones shaped like oval eggs that could fit in the palms of her hands. For a moment she thought they were eggs, but, upon picking them up, she realized they were just stones.

That's odd. I thought they looked like they were glowing before.

Nata shrugged before she trotted back over to Meeka. Meeka bent her head down with her most intent stare. Indeed, it was a wonder she didn't bore a hole through Nata's hands with her gaze. Nata didn't blame her though, they were rather stunning.

"Hold your hands up good and flat, so I can see what we have found."

"Aren't they gorgeous? So smooth and round, just like eggs."

"Oh my! They certainly are beautiful. The purple even matches my scales, but they are rather small. Put them in your travel pouch on your waist for now please, and let's get going. We do need to get back to Master Pukas's house before dark after all."

Nata nodded, and did as Meeka suggested. No sooner had she begun to reach for Meeka's horn in order to climb up the saddle, than a shudder rumbled through the ground.

—Chapter 4—

After the shudder, the sand underneath them began to cave in.

"Meeka!"

"On my back. Quick!"

With the shifting of the sand beneath them, Nata managed a rather precarious maneuver into the saddle on Meeka's back, before she saw a large brown head coming out of the sand with its mouth open wide not two lengths of Meeka's wings. Its head was four times the size of Meeka. As Meeka stretched out her wings to take off, its forked tongue snaked out, and grabbed Nata's bare wrist. With a twist of its head, the snake jerked her off Meeka. As she flew through the air, her pouch containing the ammera flower was dislodged from her shoulder, and went flying from her sight.

No! Mama needs that flower!

Nata landed with a spectacular thump in what was becoming a rather large sandpit with the snake's tongue still wrapped around her left wrist. She dug her feet into the shifting sand as best she could, reaching for anything that might help anchor her. It was a losing battle. The snake was far too big for her to pull herself free.

Wait! My knife! The tongue is soft. I bet if cut it with my knife the sand snake will let go!

New plan in place, she stopped struggling against the sand snake, and instead reached with her tail towards her knife. Venom from the snake dribbled on her wrist, and up her arm. The snake hissed as its tongue began to drag her across the sand.

Just a little more. Just a little more! There!

With a flourish of her tail, she passed the knife to her right hand, grateful that her dominant arm was not being held by the snake. Quick as lightning, she brought the knife down on the tongue holding her, and the sand snake let out a terrific hissing howl as it let go. Meeka wasted no time snarling as she flew towards the snake spouting flame from her mouth. Sensing larger prey, it changed course as it darted to grab Meeka.

The sudden shift in movement by the snake caused Nata to go sliding across the sand before she bumped into the side of the snake's neck. A deep gash covered its mottled left eye. It blew a blast of air out of the side slits on its neck into her face, sending her tumbling head over heels once more. The smell was rancid. With her eyes stinging, and struggling to contain her coughs from the horrible smell, she crawled up to the top of the sandpit.

Once clear, she dragged herself to her feet, and began to stumble away from the sand snake's trap. Some sort of luck must have been with her still in spite of everything, because she could just make out the blurred image of the pouch with the ammera flower inside, not one span of Meeka's wings from the edge of the pit. She staggered towards the pouch to scoop it up before she continued to put some distance between her and the snake. Meeka kept attacking, until she was out of its reach.

Another hiss pierced the sky, and Nata heard the beat of wings heading towards her. The snake's dark shadow seemed to reach for the suns as its tongue flickered through the air. She closed her eyes against the wave of sand Meeka kicked up as she landed right in front of her.

Before Meeka even had a chance to say anything, Nata beat her to it. "It blew something into my eyes. They're stinging."

"Don't panic. The snake blows sand into the eyes of its prey to blind them. You won't be able to flush them out with water while we are flying, so you'll have to use some water to flush them out now."

Nata nodded, and managed a half blind grasp to hurl herself into the saddle on Meeka's back. As soon as she was settled, she reached for the water skin fastened to her waist. The ground trembled as she used water from the water skin to flush the sand out of her eyes.

"Hurry!"

Once her eyes were clear, she slung the water skin around her neck, and made sure the pouch with the ammera flower was secure. "Okay, ready."

Meeka flew up towards the suns just in time, for the sand underneath them exploded as the snake shot into the air. Its tongue, moist with venom, barely missed Nata's leg.

Nata sagged in the saddle. "Whew!"

"Whew is right. That was a little too close. By the way, good job with the knife Nata, but be quick to wash your arm before the venom is absorbed into your skin. A sand snake's eyesight isn't the greatest, but its tongue can taste the air to find its prey for miles. I doubt it's going to be willing to give up on finding us if it can smell us."

Nata nodded, and set to work washing her arm. It was rather difficult to see with her eyes watering. She might have cleared out the sand, but that didn't stop her eyes from letting her know they were not happy with their sandy trauma. When she was finished cleaning her arm, she placed a poultice on her reddened skin, and wrapped some cloth around it.

She contemplated throwing the cloth she used to wash her arm down to the ground as a distraction for the snake, but then thought better of it. Her papa might be able to use the venom residue for something, so she wrapped the cloth with care, and placed it inside her travel pouch at her waist. Wounds tended and adrenaline fading, she rested her uninjured hand on Meeka's scales just as the enormity of the situation hit her.

She could see Meeka's ears flatten despite the wind. "...I'm sorry Nata. We shouldn't have stopped."

Nata patted Meeka's scales. "You're forgiven, but I think we have tempted fate enough for today. Let's hurry back to Master Pukas's house."

Time seemed to pass quickly now that they were out of immediate danger. Looking below, she saw a wondering dust devil swirl across the brown sand below them. To the left stood the dark silent trees of Narley Forest. Three black turkey vultures flew in circles high above the trees. Nata sighed as the cool wind brushed against her face. The distant mountains began to swallow both suns, with a brilliant display of colors a vibrant red, mixed with purple, pink, and blue. Dark shadows of the night crept towards them.

I hope we make it back to Master Pukas's before the suns go down.

Despite the fact that the mountain dragons don't hunt at night, there are other creatures that do. At home they were always safe in the treetops, after the twin suns went down. The location of their colony was specifically chosen to be safe from the night time hunters as long as they stayed in their trees.

One good thing about being up in the air was it gave her some time to heal. After a time, her eyes had stopped watering though they were still a bit tender. Her arm was feeling better as well, though she was sure that she was going to be a mess of bruises all over by tomorrow. Meeka's ears hadn't moved from their flattened position, and Nata thought she could do with some cheering up.

As a matter of fact, she could use some cheering up too. When things had settled down, and her eyes had quit watering so bad, she had taken a look at the ammera flower in her pouch. Just a peek of course. She didn't want to start Meeka into another sneezing fit.

The flower had taken quite a beating in their brush with the sand snake. Meeka seemed to wilt when Nata told her of the damage to the flower even as she poured more speed into their flight. Nata only hoped that enough of the flower could be salvaged, otherwise they had gone through all that work with nothing to show for it but bruises. Her tail had been involuntarily wrapping around her injured arm in her distress, and she had wrapped it around her right arm to keep the tail from adding to her left arm's injury.

In the distance, Nata spied the lake that was beside Master Pukas's house.

I hope Master Pukas can do something about the flower.

Poor Meeka. Anyone could make mistakes. They were alive to try again if they had to. She was deliberately not thinking of the fact that her mama might not have the extra day. At least, not until she knew if Master Pukas could do something about the flower. Furthermore, they would have a better idea of what to expect next time, so it wasn't a total loss. Somewhat cheered from these thoughts, she set out trying to come up with a way to cheer Meeka up before they reached Master Pukas's house.

Nata patted Meeka's scales. "Stop that silly. I told you that you were forgiven. We don't even know if the flower is a total loss until we get to Master Pukas's house, and you know what Mama would say 'Best not to borrow trouble that isn't there'."

"That's true," Meeka conceded.

Nata knew she had said the right thing as she could feel some of the coiled tension loosen in the scales beneath her hand.

Her tail uncoiled from her arm. "My arm and eyes feel better."

Meeka's ears perked up at last. "Thank goodness."

Thinking about her arm and eyes, lead her to thinking about their encounter with the sand snake. Meeka had seen sand snakes before, but Nata wondered how the one they faced today compared to the others Meeka had seen. Nata did not remember the stories of sand snakes being quite so large, but then she forgot all about the sand in the eyes trick too with the adrenaline of the moment.

Curious, with a fireheart of wisdom conveniently present, Nata decided to do a little information fishing. "That was one gigantic sand snake."

Meeka bobbed her head. "It was the biggest one I've ever seen!"

At that point, Master Pukas's house was in sight with the sorcerer in question outside by the well. From this distance, it looked like he was cranking the handle to bring water up. With a change to the beat of her wings, Meeka started to fly lower. It wasn't long before Meeka landed half a wingspan from the well with a pair of very intent eyes watching them.

Master Pukas looked directly at Nata with his eyebrows raised clear up into his braided hair cap. "Well, I see that you did not come back by way of Narley Forest. I was beginning to think the mountain dragons had gotten the better of you."

Nata flushed before she began opening her mouth to reply, but Meeka raised one of her wings in front of Nata as if to shield her from the sorcerer's scrutiny.

Meeka huffed when Master Pukas switched his gaze to her eyes. "Well, yes. You see Master Pukas, I underestimated the pungent smell of the ammera flowers. I tell you, I did a lot of sneezing. After an especially explosive sneeze, I was concerned that we had woken up something we shouldn't have, so we took another way home. We stopped at the oasis on the way, because I was in need of a drink from all the sneezing. Also a sand snake attacked us, so on the whole, I would say that we had quite an adventurous day."

Master Pukas frowned. "I didn't know a sand snake lived close to the oasis."

Meeka flexed her wings in her approximation of a shrug. "We stopped on a sand dune after we left the oasis to look at a trifle."

"Hmm...," Master Pukas stroked his goatee.

Nata leaned forwards in the saddle so she could catch Master Pukas's eyes from behind Meeka's wing. "Umm..., Master Pukas?"

Master Pukas's eyes turned towards Nata, and she fought not to shrink back behind Meeka's wing. "May we stay the night?"

"Ye gads girl," Master Pukas exclaimed. "What kind of a monster do you think I am? Of course you may stay the night. In fact, I insist. I was more concerned about how to convince you to stay the night, since you seem so keen on doing things on your own despite the risk, and your youth."

Nata blushed. "Oh…"

"Contrary to the impression you seem to have of me. One of my jobs is to protect my fellow elbees. I cannot do that when they are rushing headlong into things. If you had waited before you charged off like you did, I would have told you I would have taken Arrow in the morning as Meeka would have been unaccustomed to the smell, and it was too late in the day to make it there and back today. I would have been back by late afternoon tomorrow, and you could have made it home by tomorrow evening. Nomo did not send you with a message of extra haste, so I doubt a few more hours to get the flower to Nami would have made that much difference."

Nata shrank down in the saddle with a bright red face.

Master Pukas sighed. "But the two of you were also very brave. May I see the flower?"

Nata slipped off Meeka, and presented the pouch that held ammera flower to Master Pukas. "We got the flower, but it got damaged in the fight with the sand snake."

Master Pukas accepted the pouch, and glanced at the bandages on her left arm. "Didn't escape unscathed I see."

Nata's tail drooped as she tried to make

herself as small as possible. "It's not that bad..."

Master Pukas shook his head. "I'll have a look at it anyway once we get inside my house. Would that Shea'a were here. My skills at healing are paltry in comparison to hers. Now, let me see about this flower..."

Oh Shea'a! Papa has told me stories of her before. She was a healer sorceress, but I haven't heard a story about her for some time. I thought she was just a fictional character.

Without further ado, Master Pukas reached towards the pouch to open it.

Meeka flapped her wings in agitation. "For goodness sake don't open that right now! How in Aquatia can you even stand the smell?"

Master Pukas's reply was as dry as dust. "You can thank my sister for that."

Both Meeka and Nata looked at Master Pukas in confusion.

Master Pukas rolled his eyes, while his hair started to braid in all directions the way it had when Nata first met him. "In our youth, she *insisted* that she knew a spell to enhance the sense of smell. Unfortunately, I was lucky target that got to be her guinea pig. Needless, to say the spell backfired rather spectacularly, and now I am left with no sense of smell at all. I am fortunate that it does come in handy for some situations."

Meeka and Nata were both following his

hair's sentient, haphazard braiding with wide eyes during his rant. Seeing as he had somewhat lost the attention of his audience, Master Pukas humphed, grabbed the bucket full of water with the hand not occupied by the pouch, and headed back towards the house.

His tail was lashing through the air, and his hair was still weaving odd braided shapes, while he grumbled under his breath. "She still has not managed to figure out how to give me my sense of smell back. Not even after all these years."

"Meeka…," Nata whispered. "What is up with his hair?"

Meeka flared her wings. "I have no idea. I've never seen it do that before."

Meeka sniffed, and followed the old sorcerer into his house. Nata took one look at the forest before she followed them. Just as she reached the door to go into the house, she glanced again into the forest where she saw blue, green, and red bulbous eyes shining back at her. Her tail and all the fur on it stood on end as she dashed into the house, and shut the door with a loud slam.

—Chapter 5—

Meeka sniffed. "Nata! Why did you shut the door like that? You almost caught my tail!"

"Sorry Meeka, but I saw about a hundred eyes of different colors peering at me out of the forest. It frightened me."

"Hmph!" Meeka shuffled over beside the fireplace, where she promptly curled up in a heap. Soon soft rumbles gurgled out her mouth, and tendrils of smoke came out of her nostrils.

Nata sighed as she sat down beside Master Pukas, who was sitting in one of two chairs by the fire. There was a small table between them that was a little way back from the fire. It had some food on it as well as some medical supplies.

"Nata, let me have a look at your arm."

"I washed and applied a poultice to it."

Master Pukas sent her an exasperated look. "Let me check it anyway please."

Nata blushed. She felt a bit sheepish as she remembered his earlier concern, and held out her arm for him to inspect. He unwrapped the cloth bandage to reveal that underneath the bandage her skin showed just a hint of pink.

Nata watched his tail droop as he reapplied a poultice, and wrapped a clean cloth around it again. She wondered why her wound made him sad, then she remembered him talking about Shea'a. It was just a guess, but Nata figured that binding the wound was reminding him of her.

I guess Shea'a isn't just a story, but… I wonder why no one talks about her.

"Well, your arm should be mended by morning. You had best have a bite to eat, and then get some sleep."

Nata ducked her head. "What about the flower?"

"While you get some sleep, I'll take a look at it. I know the initial preparation stages of the flower for the medicine that Nomo plans to make. If we are lucky, the flower will be in good enough shape I can get the flower into that form, which would make it easier for Nomo anyway as it will be ready to use. It also has the advantage of not losing its potency for quite some time."

Nata's shoulders slumped. "Oh..."

"If not, I will go retrieve another flower tomorrow."

Nata breathed out in relief. "Thank you."

"The parts of the flower used in the medicine are quite hardy. I am fairly certain I should have no problems. Please get some rest. I am optimistic that you will be on your way back to the colony early tomorrow."

Nata nodded as she reached out, and grabbed the food on the table. Thankfully, it was not more of that dreadful stuff she had to eat before. Instead it was corn crackers, fish, and cheese. All of the sudden she realized she was quite ravenous, but also rather tired as well.

She devoured the offered food with relish, but the full stomach only added to her feeling of lethargy. The floor next to Meeka looked inviting, so she curled up underneath one of Meeka's wings. Just as she was falling asleep, it occurred to her that Meeka must have slept here before.

Nata woke up with a start, and sat up. She was in an unfamiliar room. The firelight cast dancing shadows about the quiet room, despite the sunlight streaming in from the windows.

Wha—

Oh that's right. I'm at Master Pukas's house, but... where's Meeka?

...Well first things first.

On the table where she had eaten dinner the night before, sat a mug of water, wedge of cheese, bread, and tark roots. Her brain still hadn't quite woken up yet, but she was startled to realize there was a blanket that had slipped off her shoulders when she had woken up. A tiny smile graced her face.

Master Pukas must have covered me with a blanket while I slept.

Not wanting to be a bad guest, she folded the blanket before she placed it neatly on the chair. Breakfast smelled delicious, but first she wanted to check her bandage. When she removed the bandage her skin was still a little irritated, so she rewrapped the injury.

If things went well, she could have Papa look at it when she got home, just to be sure. Not that she didn't trust Master Pukas, but he had said healing wasn't his forte. Better safe than sorry in this case. Arm attended to she turned to the food, and ate with gusto. She was so relieved that the horrible excuse for a first meal was not repeated.

Maybe that's just the way he eats when no one

is here, and he saves food like this for guests? But that doesn't make sense, because there would have been no way for him to get food so fast. Whatever the reason, if he eats food like that first meal when no one is here, is that really all that good for his health?

Once she finished her breakfast, and gathered up her things, she looked around for her pouch that held the flower in it. She hoped that enough of the flower had been salvageable.

The pouch was nowhere to be seen.

Oh no! Did Master Pukas have to go get another flower?

She could think of no other reason why both her pouch, and Master Pukas weren't present. Come to think of it, Meeka wasn't here either.

Maybe Master Pukas took Meeka to go get another flower since she proved she can handle the smell?

I suppose I can go see if anyone is outside.

Nata felt the muscles in her tail uncoil as soon as she opened the door to Master Pukas's house. Outside, Meeka was curled up on the ground beside the lake. She cracked open an eye as soon as Nata shut Master Pukas's front door.

"There you are! You finally woke up. I was going to wake you up earlier. Master Pukas said that we should leave when the suns started to rise this morning, but I fell asleep. Did you see the breakfast set out for you?"

Nata stretched and yawned. "Yes, I ate the breakfast, but where is Master Pukas?"

"He said he had something to check out, so he left way before the suns rose this morning. He left your pouch, with the flower ingredient inside, tied to my saddle."

Nata peered around Meeka's side, and sure enough there was her pouch. The knowledge that he had no trouble preparing the flower left her dizzy with relief. She untied the pouch from Meeka's saddle, and placed it over her shoulder before reaching in to check the contents. There was a small jar inside.

Meeka nudged her shoulder. "Do you have everything?"

"Yes."

"We had best be going then. I am afraid that my nap will cause us trouble later."

Nata reached up, grabbed Meeka's horn, and climbed onto her back. Up into the air Meeka flew, heading for home as fast as she could.

"Meeka, do you know what Master Pukas was checking out?"

"I have no idea."

"I was just wondering..."

"Wondering will do you no good, because he's not here to ask."

"But..." Nata sighed. "Okay."

"We need to keep a sharp eye out, and stay alert. Master Pukas thinks that we could have trouble on the way home."

The suns, Pa and Na, were bright balls of yellow fire. It was an indication that it was going to be a hot day. Normally, Nata would have enjoyed a day like today, but she felt the fingers of dread tingle up her spine. They flew along quietly, both of them looking around and listening for the slightest of sounds. Their dark shadows raced across the murky green lake below.

Nata was worried. If trouble came, they would have nowhere to hide. She could feel Meeka exerting herself to get to the other side of Whyttle Lake as fast as possible. It felt like they had been flying forever, but she reasoned to herself that it was the tension getting to her. Her neck was starting to get stiff from looking around, when she started hearing a faint buzzing sound in her ear. Nata put her hands up to her neck, and rubbed it to see if that would make the sound go away.

Suddenly, Meeka's head snapped around. Nata could see her eyes go wide before she dove towards the lake. With a gasp, Nata used her claws to grab ahold of the saddle to keep from falling off. They spiraled down to the lake until she thought they would splash into it. Just before they hit the lake, Meeka leveled off so that her claws barely skimmed the surface, and started furiously flapping her wings.

The strange buzz in her ears was getting louder and louder. Meeka was flying so fast now that it was all she could do to hang on. She latched her tail onto the saddle for some extra support. Meeka had heard or smelled something she was sure. Nata only hoped that it wasn't a mountain dragon.

They were almost to the other side of the lake, when a dark speck loomed behind them. Instead of flying towards home, Meeka changed directions. The change in direction didn't seem to help. Every second that passed, caused the dark speck to get closer. Just when Nata thought she couldn't hold on any longer, Meeka slowed down. This allowed her to loosen her hold just enough to let the blood flow back into her numb hands and arms.

Where are we going?

Soon they were across the lake, flying over the grasses. Red, yellow, pink, and purple flowers blended into the landscape. A startled herd of lambeos scattered across the grasses, and the occasional birdcall shattered the stillness. She looked towards the dark speck, and was dismayed when it began to take the shape of a dragon. In the distance ahead, Nata could distinguish some dark round shapes that seemed to be their destination.

If Meeka was looking for a place to hide, why didn't she fly into the forest?

A distant roar sent a chill down her spine.

Meeka flew low. Nata could clearly see dark

grey mounds, covered with moss and lichen. Some were big, and some were small. Meeka landed, and faced a large grey mound with vines hanging down covering most of it. As Meeka walked to the mound, Nata could feel her sides heaving. Meeka's breath was coming in labored gasps. This added to Nata's apprehension as she glanced around.

Why did Meeka think they could hide here?

The buzzing noise was becoming deafening in her ears, but now it sounded like a song. A song she had never heard before.

Meeka stopped in front of the mound. *"Danomme."*

Nata heard the word, a crack, and a snap just above the strange song in her ears. To her amazement, the outline of a door appeared on the smooth surface of the mound that slid open with a grating sound. She clung to Meeka as she scrambled inside, and the door shut with a snap as a loud roar sounded behind them.

—Chapter 6—

The whole reveal and entrance into the odd room happened so fast that she didn't have time to comprehend it. Not to mention, the singing in her ears was so loud now that she clapped her hands over her ears in an attempt to mute it. Meeka was crouched low on the ground with Nata still on her back.

Before long, Nata's eyes adjusted to the gloom, and she glanced around the peculiar place. She wasn't sure what to call it. There was a small waterfall at the far end. At the top of the door, a small opening was chiseled out of the rock. Light filtered in through the vines outside giving them just a bit of light.

For what seemed like hours, Meeka and Nata stayed very still. Over the course of the time they spent waiting, the loud singing in her ears died down to a mild buzzing sound.

Meeka finally stirred. "I think the danger has passed for now, but we mustn't let our guard down."

"Meeka, was that a mountain dragon?"

"Yes, I do believe it was."

"Oh," Nata's tail curled around her wrist. "Why do the mountain dragons dislike us?"

"According to the stories, they didn't always. Nobody really knows why that changed. At least nobody has ever said why."

Nata frowned as she glanced around. "What is this place?"

Meeka flexed her wings. "It's called Drall Mounds, and sand dragons have used it as a hiding place for a long time. Sand dragons are taught the opening phrase, and the mounds location from a young age."

Nata chewed on her lip. "Oh."

Meeka ambled over to the pool of water to take a drink. "My wings need a rest. Then we will slip out of the mound, and fly home. My wings are no match for the power of a mountain dragon. Their wings are bigger and stronger. Oh, why did I fall asleep this morning!"

Nata slid off of Meeka's back, and rubbed her

hands together. They were as cold as stones. There was still a faint buzzing sound in her ears. After taking a cool drink from her water skin, she reached towards the pouch on her belt for some bread and cheese.

When she opened her pouch, a faint purple glow emitted from it. Nata gasped. The egg-shaped stones they had found in the sands cast an eerie purple light around the room.

"My word," Meeka licked her lips.

Nata's eyes were as round as saucers, and Meeka was staring speechlessly at her pouch. The stones were cool to the touch as she took them out,

and held them in her hands. "Why do you suppose the stones are glowing?"

"I am not sure, but put them back in your pouch please. It would not do for a purple glow to be coming out of the mound. No telling what kind of trouble that would bring."

Looking around with sudden apprehension, Nata put the stones away. She took the pouch containing the flower extract off of her shoulder. Meeka lay down to rest as she sat down on the stone floor, and munched on her snack.

Boy! I can't wait until we get home. I am going to tell Nole about everything that has happened to Meeka and I.

Nole and Nata had been best friends since they were very small, usually they went everywhere together. This had been the first time he was needed during the hunting season.

I wonder if the colony knows about the mountain dragon?

"Meeka do you think everyone left at the Elbano Colony is going to be all right? With the sand dragons out hunting, will they even hear a mountain dragon?"

"Really Nata, Dree did not go hunting. He is too old, you know. Although his hearing and sense of smell are not in prime condition, he can hear well enough to distinguish the sounds and type of dragon approaching."

Nata slumped. "You're right."

"And besides the colony is well hidden from

mountain dragons."

"Thanks Meeka. That makes me feel better."

"Anytime," Meeka sniffed. "Do you have some liniment in your pouch? I am afraid my wings are getting quite stiff."

Nata opened the pouch on her belt, which contained herbs and liniment. "The stones aren't glowing anymore."

"Hmm…, that is peculiar."

She sighed in relief, grateful that the odd buzzing and song had stopped. After she climbed onto Meeka's back, Nata gently rubbed the liniment onto Meeka's soft leathery wings as she flexed them.

"Meeka, how long do you think we have been here? The suns do not seem to be shining in through the holes quite as bright."

"Quite right you are. It is starting to get late into the day. We can leave as soon as this liniment helps my muscles loosen up."

Nata went over to the waterfall with the pool at its base. Resting on her knees, Nata put her water skin bag into the pool to fill it up, and watched as ripples race across the pool. Something yellow glinted in the dim light. She dipped the claw on her hand into the cool water, and sent a large ripple across the top of the water again.

"Nata, what are you doing?"

"There's something in the pool."

Nata leaned forward, stretched her hand out to grab whatever it was in the pool, and nearly fell in.

"Nata, do be careful."

"I'm being careful. Don't worry so much."

Meeka was quivering with excitement. "It taste like gold."

Her red forked tongue darted out, and slipped beneath the pool's surface.

"You can taste it?"

"Any dragon worth their armored scales can taste gold. It's a rich flavor of gold too. You can climb up on my neck to see if you can reach it."

"Okay." Once up on Meeka's neck, she reached into the pool, and pulled out a gold cup with two dragon tail handles.

"Hop down, and let me look at it please."

Sitting beside the pool, Nata lightly ran her hands over the cup's cool surface using her claws to pick some grime out of the crevices. The heavy round cup was twice the size of the drinking gourds the colony used. Spiked dragon tails were wrapped around its handles.

Meeka's eyes glistened in the dim light. "The cup would make a nice addition to my collection."

Nata giggled. "You can add the cup to your hoard, but how did it get in the pool to begin with?"

"Bah," Meeka snorted. "Who knows? Maybe

another dragon found a stash of treasure, and lost it when they used the mound as a hiding place on their way home."

Nata blinked. "Huh, that would make sense."

"Could you wrap it up before you put it in your pouch? That way the jar with the ammera flower extract won't damage it, and keep it from making noise."

"Good plan." Nata wrapped the cup up, put it in the pouch, and then she nestled the jar with the ammera flower extract in the cup to keep it from being jostled.

Just then a loud rumble came from Meeka's stomach, causing Nata to laugh.

Meeka sniffed. "Well, you try and go without any food, and see if your stomach doesn't start to rumble. All that I have eaten today is thirty blue fish, and that was hours ago. I'm fair famished, but there is no time for me to eat now. Besides, I think my wings are rested up enough to fly us home."

"Sorry Meeka. I did not mean to laugh at you. I am worried about getting home tonight as well. I don't fancy being a dragon's dinner, but the thought of flying at night is scarier."

"Well, yes, I can see your point. However, I have no intention of our being anyone's dinner. Let's try to be as quiet as possible on the way home."

"Okay Meeka."

She climbed up onto Meeka's back, and Meeka lumbered over to the door.

"*Da-nomme*," she commanded.

There was a crack, a snap, and then the door slid open. Up into the air they flew once more, and, by looking at the suns, she knew that Meeka was right. It would be well into the night before they arrived home.

Oh dear. This trip has been one mess after another. I never thought I would wish for a mountain dragon to be hunting us, but the night hunters are even worse.

Here's hoping we find our way home safely without any mishaps.

Meeka flew up high enough to catch her wind breeze, at least that is what she called it. The wind breeze pushes her along, allowing her to expend less energy to fly.

It was getting close to dusk. The suns were merging into a single orange disk in the sky, giving off just enough hint of color, and promising a spectacular sunset. Nata clutched the purple horn on Meeka's neck with both hands while she glanced around. She looked down at Windle Forest on her left, the grass below, and to Whyttle Lake on the right.

They had been flying for about an hour when it finally dawned on her. It was quiet, too quiet in fact. The skies were empty of any dragons, mountain dragons or otherwise, and they hadn't seen one animal since they had left Drall Mounds.

She had never been out flying at night before. Beside the higher risk level, no one had ever mentioned just how eerie it was. How Nata wished that looking behind her didn't give her neck such a crick. The thought of a something coming up behind them was so scary that she shivered, and nearly fell off.

Nata's sudden movement was enough to cause Meeka to glance back at her.

This is not good.

Stop thinking and pay attention to what is going on, or you will fall off if Meeka goes into another sudden dive.

The sky that had been a brilliant display of color was now beginning to fade into night. The moons and stars started to dominate the edge of a night sky. In the twilight, the landscape was just beginning to become familiar to her when she noticed a faint buzzing sound in her ears again.

Oh! No! Not again. Maybe I am having a delayed reaction to the ammera flower? But how could that be?

Nata was just grateful the buzzing sound didn't get any louder. Darkness was covering the sky now, and the stars were beautiful in the heavens. She had never seen them with such an unobstructed view before. It was such a shame that the night hunters kept them from this view all the time.

"Hang on Nata."

She felt Meeka's muscles bunch, and her wings flapped furiously.

Now what?

A sudden chill invaded her body. The moons Panos and Nanos rode high in the sky casting dark shadows below them. The air was cool, but it had nothing to do with the chill in her. The buzzing sound was becoming clear enough to distinguish a lilting musical melody again. Just then, Meeka went into a dive towards the ground, and Nata could see the dark blur of elban trees rushing up to meet them. Meeka pulled up just above them, high enough to miss the treetops.

Suddenly, she knew they were almost home. They flew along for a little longer before Meeka slipped silently into her dark lair. Home at last, and safe from the predators that rule Aquatia's night. They had made it without becoming a dragon's dinner, or anything else's dinner for that matter. Meeka's heavy breathing was the only sound she heard. It was so dark that she could not see Meeka's neck in front of her, although she still held onto her neck horn with both hands.

Well, my eyes have to adjust to the darkness before I can climb down. Otherwise, I will find myself in a dilly of a mess.

The buzzing sound that had been plaguing her off and on the whole trip seemed to fade away. Without warning, Meeka stirred from where she had been crouched, and moved further into her lair. This time Nata was holding on so that she did not take her by surprise.

It was then that she remembered what her papa had said, "When on a dragon's back it is wise to always hold on, and expect the unexpected."

Thoughts of her papa and mama brought a lump into her throat, and tears to her eyes.

I hope Mama is going to be all right.

Nata's eyes had finally adjusted enough for her to make out the table along the wall. From the smell, she would say there were fish and berries on it. She could see the outline of Meeka's wooden water gourd, and the center of the room. Finally, Nata felt safe enough to climb down. She was just about to do so, when her ears heard a soft scraping noise coming from the doorway that led into their house.

—Chapter 7—

Meeka tensed. Nata glanced up and saw a black shape looming in the doorway.

"Eek!" She crashed down onto the floor.

"Nata?" The yellow glow of candlelight shone on Papa's face.

"Papa," Nata ran into his arms as tears started to slide down her face. "Papa."

"It's alright Nata. You are safe now. But what in Aquatia made you think it was a good idea to travel at night?"

Nata sniffed as she wiped the tears from her eyes. "We were at Drall Mounds hiding from a mountain dragon. Once the danger had passed, we were in a hurry to get home."

Papa sighed. "Did you have any luck with the flower?"

Nata nodded. "I got some extract that Master Pukas made when I found him a flower."

Papa stopped moving, and looked down at her. "Found?"

"Um...," Nata scuffed her feet. "Master Pukas was out of the flower, so Meeka and I went to find one. It got a little damaged on the return trip. Master Pukas made it into an extract."

Papa took a deep breath. "Well that will make the preparation of the medicine faster, but why didn't you let Master Pukas go get a flower?"

Nata blushed so hard that even in the dim light you could see it. "I panicked?"

Papa glanced at Meeka.

Meeka shrugged. "I was worried about Mama too."

Papa slumped. "Flying at night, and going close to the Dark Mountains. I swear you two just shaved years off my life."

"Sorry," both Meeka and Nata whispered.

Papa's tail wrapped around his waist. "Frankly, I'm afraid to ask about the bandage on your arm."

Nata winced. "Sand snake."

Papa closed his eyes. "Of course."

"It's not that bad," Nata protested. "Master Pukas checked it already. I just thought it might be better to let you check it too. We were flying still, and I thought the extra protection might be a good thing."

Papa chuckled. "I won't worry too much then, but I am pleased to see your healer instincts. Dare I ask if there is anything else you need to warn my poor old heart about?

Nata hesitated. "Master Pukas's hair does some weird braiding... thing?"

Papa outright snickered. "Yes. Yes it does."

Nata pouted. "You could have warned me."

"Where would have been the fun in that." Papa grinned, and ruffled her hair. "At least you are both safe. Come with me please Nata. You can help me make the medicine for Mama. It will be a good experience in your training."

Nata nodded. "Is Mama going to be alright?"

"Yes, she should be fine now that we have the ammera flower extract to make her medicine."

As Papa turned to go into the house, Nata glanced at Meeka.

She ran over to Meeka, and pressed her lips against her scaly neck. "Thanks for getting us home in one piece."

Meeka sniffed. "You're welcome, but next time don't crash down onto the floor, and give me a scare. Please don't forget about my cup either."

"Okay Meeka." Nata giggled as she pulled the cup out of her pouch. She took care to remove the jar with the flower extract, and place it back in the pouch. The cup she unwrapped before she placed it beside a gold plate.

Nata dashed after her papa towards the house. A glance back just before she went inside made her smile. Meeka was enjoying a feast of fish and berries that Papa had set out for her.

Their treehouse home consisted of one room. In the center of the wall at the far end of the room, was a stone fireplace used for cooking. On one side of the fireplace sat a huge clay pot, cooking utensils, and a stack of fire wood. The other side of the fireplace had the beds with a small table in-between them. The left wall was lined with shelves filled with books, bowls, containers used for eating, and earthenware pots of all shapes, sizes, and colors. These pots were filled with leaves, herbs, and powders used by Papa to make medicine. There was a long table with a bench along the other wall.

The soft yellow glow of candlelight reflected on Mama's face. Her breathing was so soft as to be barely noticeable. Nata could see the sweat on her brow from across the room as she handed Papa the pouch with the extract in it.

Papa placed the pouch on the table, and took

out the flower extract. "That's a significant amount of extract. How big was that flower you found for Master Pukas?"

"It filled up the pouch with little room to spare. Meeka had to cut it with her claw. Otherwise, I would not have been able to get it as my knife would not cut through the stem. The flower made Meeka sneeze a lot, and that almost burned the flower too."

"My goodness that sounds like a huge flower! With this much extract, I should be able to make enough of the medicines it uses for a long time," he whispered with a pleased smile.

Nata's tail curled in the air. "That's great."

Papa nodded. "Yes it is. Nata, would you please bring me the big bowl off the shelf."

"Yes Papa."

Papa gathered a bunch of ingredients from the shelves for the medicine while she got the bowl. "So... Meeka found a gold cup to add to her hoard."

Nata giggled. "Papa, I think Meeka is attracted to bright shiny objects, especially gold."

Papa chuckled as his black eyes twinkled. "Dragons are fond of treasures. Come here, and help me prepare these please."

Nata hopped up on a stool, and started assisting her papa. The two of them cut, and ground the various roots, herbs, and extracts into a smooth mixture in the bowl. Her papa used his tail to pick up the ingredients, while he used his hands to steady the bowl as he stirred. He added only a few drops of the ammera flower extract to the mixture.

"There, all we need now is the cricket berry juice. Nata, could you please bring me the pot with the juice in it? I need to keep stirring this, or it will turn out wrong."

Nata scurried to fetch the pot. "Yes Papa."

She thought she had a good grip on the pot, but apparently her hands were sweaty from nerves. The pot slid right out of her hands, and down to the floor. It was a good thing the pot was rather sturdy, because it didn't break. All the same, the noise it made when it hit the ground was rather loud, and most of the contents spilled out all over the floor before it rolled upright.

Nata went white as a sheet.

Oh no! I know that the cricket berries aren't quite as rare an ingredient as the ammera flower extract, but they are no less important.

"Breathe Nata," Papa's voice was gentle as he broke through her horror. "It was an accident. It's going to be okay. Just pick the pot up for now, and bring it here please. I'll bet there is enough in the bottom to make this dose of medicine at least."

Nata gulped, and her tail wrapped around her waist. With shaking hands, she reached down to pick the pot off the floor, and carried it gingerly over to her papa. He favored her with a bright smile as he added some of the juice to the mixture, and then some water. His stirring had never stopped, and the end result had just the right consistency.

"There we go. Just right." Papa smiled. "Now we are ready to give Mama some medicine. I'll carry the medicine, while you carefully carry the candle."

Nata nodded, and together they walked over to Mama's bed. She put the candle down beside the bed.

Papa held the bowl out towards her. "Here, hold the bowl of medicine for me please."

"But—"

"It'll be okay."

Nata's hands shook as she accepted the bowl full of medicine. Papa filled the wooden spoon with some medicine, and let the liquid slowly trickle down Mama's throat. Spoonful by spoonful, the medicine vanished from the bowl, and the longer Nata held the bowl without dropping it the less her hands shook. After about half the medicine was gone, he took a cloth, and wiped the sweat off of Mama's flushed round face. Nata put the bowl filled with the rest of the medicine down before she tucked the damped strands of Mama's blonde hair behind her pointed ears.

Mama stirred and whispered. "Nata?"

"I'm here Mama. Papa gave you some medicine, so now you will get better."

She breathed a faint sigh, and drifted back

into a restless sleep.

Papa picked up the bowl with the rest of the medicine, and took it back to the mixing table. "Well that's a good sign at least. Don't worry too much Nata, your mama is a strong woman. Now, let's have a look see at that wrist you have bandaged before you get some sleep."

Nata yawned. "Okay Papa."

He reached over, and unwrapped her arm. "Hmm... it's seems to be mending nicely. Probably won't even be pink tomorrow. I think you can go ahead, and leave the bandage off for tonight. I will clean up the mess. You have had a busy two days, and I am sure you are very tired. Let me tuck you into bed."

Hand in hand, they walked over to her bed, where Papa tucked her in, and kissed her forehead. "My brave Nata, I'm very proud of you."

"Thanks Papa."

As she was drifting off to sleep, she remembered the stones they had found, and the strange song she had heard. She had forgotten to tell Papa about them. It would have to wait until tomorrow, because the excitement of the day had left her exhausted.

With her eyes closed, she could hear the door open, and the tell-tale sound of scales moving through the room to her customary spot in front of the fireplace. Soon she could hear Meeka's soft rumbles, and her warm breath that warded off the chill of the night. It wasn't even a half a minute before she fell into a sound sleep.

Nata awoke the next morning, and glanced over at Mama. Papa had her propped up, so that she could drink more medicine from the wooden bowl. He glanced over at Nata, and winked. She watched Mama while she drank, relieved to see that she could sit up in bed.

"Yuck," Mama grumbled after she handed the empty bowl back to Papa.

Papa chuckled. "Might not taste too good Mama, but see how much better you feel already.

"Yes Papa," she sighed.

"Look Mama, Nata's awake."

"Nata," Mama smiled at her.

Nata hopped out of bed, and went over to her mama's side. Mama reached, out and clasped her hand.

"Mama, are you feeling better?"

"Yes, Nata, I'm feeling a little better, but very weak and tired. Papa said that you have been very busy helping him."

Nata smiled. "Yes Mama."

Mama was going to be okay.

Nata could see that Mama was struggling to stay awake. Her eyes kept closing, and she would doze off for a second or two. The effort of staying awake finally overcame her, and with a soft sigh she drifted off to sleep. Nata gently took her hand, and placed it back under the covers.

After making sure her mama was comfortable, Nata took out the white, clay wash bowl kept under the table by their beds, and washed her face and hands. A glance at her arm revealed that it was completely healed up from the encounter with the sand snake. She could smell the aroma of corn muffins and fish in the air. Mrs. Simo must have dropped it off for them as she knew how fond Nata was of her cooking. Nata sat down at the table, and had her fill of the fish and corn muffins.

Out of the corner of her eye, she watched Papa carefully prepare a travel pouch.

—Chapter 8—

*N*ata tilted her head in confusion. "Papa are you going on a trip?"

"No, I can't leave Mama yet. The worst is over, but it will be a week before she can be left unattended. She could recover faster with more medicine. I was hoping you could make a trip to the Mere Marshes to gather some cricket berries to make cricket berry juice. Unfortunately, Master Pukas told Meeka he was going to be gone for some time, which is why you cannot simply get the juice from him."

Nata felt the sting of tears, and hunched over.

Papa stopped packing, crossed the room, and

enveloped her in a gentle hug. "Nata, hey look at me Nata. It's okay. It was an accident. You're a healer these kinds of things are going to happen when you least want them too."

Nata's tail curled around her wrist. "Okay."

"That's my girl. We won't even go into how many accidents I had when I was learning shall we?" Papa winked. "Now, I wouldn't consider sending you to the marshes as the mere crawlers can be rather dangerous, but you proved that you could handle yourself in getting the ammera flower. The mere crawlers aren't usually a problem when I gather the cricket berries anyway, so I am not too worried. If you are going, when Meeka gets back you need to be ready to go."

"Yes, Papa. I'll go."

Wide-awake now, she watched as Papa moved back across the room, and finished packing. Inside the travel pouch he placed food, several strings, and a rope.

"The big skin pouches are for the berries. Please put your pouch full of healing herbs on your belt as well as your knife. I am also going to get a bow, quiver of arrows, and a spear ready for you to take today."

Nata blinked. "Why? I thought you said the mere crawlers wouldn't be a problem."

"Yes, but it is always better to be safe than sorry."

On the left of the entryway were two chests. The smaller chest contained knives of all shapes and sizes, a quiver with arrows, and an ax. Leaning on the wall beside the chests was a bow, a spear, and rawhide ropes in different sizes and lengths.

"Papa, what about the mountain dragons?"

"Meeka, can hear a dragon in plenty of time for you to find a place to hide. I wish Nole were here so that he could go with you, but the hunters will not be back for a few more days."

"Okay Papa."

Meeka had slipped into the room while Papa had been talking to Nata. "Are you ready to go?"

"Ready," She grabbed her pouches, bow, and placed the quiver of arrows on her shoulder. Once outside, she climbed up onto Meeka's back. Papa waited until she was settled to hand her the spear.

"Safe winds you two."

"Dragon keep you Papa."

Meeka flew high up into the air. It was a beautiful day. Nata inhaled the scent of flowers and the grasses. A distant quetzal's shriek made her shudder. Below them she glimpsed a blur of animals moving. Puffs of white and grey clouds spun shadows across the landscape. Upon further study of the clouds, it looked like it was going to rain. She hoped that by the time it rained, they would be out of the marshes.

"Meeka, I've never been to the Mere Marshes.

What are they like?"

"Well, the marshes are on the southwestern end of Whyttle Lake, near Master Pukas's house. Like any marsh it is full of water, and all sorts of plant life. The shores of the marsh hills have the best places to gather cricket berries that the nartals eat."

"What are nartals?"

"Nartals are about twice the size of a sand dragon. They are covered in long fur, spend most of their time wading on all fours through the marshes looking for food, and have a set of arms on their upper neck to pull plants down to eat. Their fur sticks out into thick spines as a defense when they sense danger is near. They are also the preferred food of the mere crawler, which is what I am worried about."

"I thought Papa said that the mere crawlers shouldn't be a problem?"

Meeka grimaced. "They shouldn't, but the way our luck has been lately, I wouldn't be too sure. You are also trained as a healer not a hunter even if you do know basic defense."

"I remember the stories about the mere crawlers that inhabit the marshes. They are supposed to have a round shell, four pairs of legs with a set of pincers for arms, and two tails that end in a group of tentacles. Their bulbous eyes are set into the shell with another mass of tentacles around their mouth."

"That's right. Their eye sight is one of their greatest weaknesses, since they can only face the one direction. We will have to be on our guard as they like to hide underwater while stalking their prey. They tend to come at you from behind, and drag you down into the marshes. Don't forget to watch out for their tentacles. They sting, and have serrated suckers."

"Are the marshes named after them?"

"Yes, and it's the only place cricket berries grow that we know of. I will search for a large hill that looks safe to land on. Hopefully, the nartals haven't eaten all the berries there yet, or we'll have to try another hill."

Nata sighed. "Let's hope good hunting favors us for a change."

The sky seemed to be alive with birds flying from one place to another in their search for food to feed their young. She watched the birds with fascination, while scouting for any signs of trouble. Straight ahead she spotted the edge of the lake with a green haze hovering just past the shore line. In no time at all, they were flying through the haze.

Nata clamped a hand over her nose. "Meeka, that smell, where is it coming from?"

Meeka snorted. "That's the marshes. We should be able to see them soon. How do you like the smell?"

"It's awful Meeka. Believe me, I will be quick."

"Good. Now I need to listen, and look carefully around before we can land."

As Meeka flew low over several hills in the marsh, Nata spied nartals all over the shores of the hills. She could see why they would need the arms to pull down the plants as they had hardly any neck at all. While she was distracted by the nartals, Meeka must have spied a hill she thought was suitable.

Soon enough they were circling a hill that was free of nartals. Meeka circled the hill three times, before she landed in the middle. It was a nice round hill. Not too steep, but with plenty of room for Meeka to land. Some luck was with them as there were plenty of cricket berry bushes, full of berries, growing close to the water. Nata climbed off of Meeka's back, and put her food pouch, and spear on the ground. She kept the pouches for the berries on her shoulder.

Meeka nuzzled Nata's arm. "I'll keep watch while you pick the berries."

She nodded at Meeka, and they started walking down the hill. Meeka walked with gentle steps, so that she would not make any noise putting her feet down. Nata followed with her eyes scanning the swamp for any signs of a mere crawler.

So far so good.

Once they reached the edge of the water, she started to pick the berries as fast as she could put them into the pouches. The quiet of the marsh was broken by the distant sound of the nartals eating cricket berries on the shores of other hills, the crickets that made their homes in the cricket berry bush, and other creatures that lived in the marsh. The second pouch was just about full when she heard Meeka snort.

"Nata, get behind me, and be careful not to make noise as you walk to the top of the hill."

Before she could move, out of the water came a huge round creature with two eyes protruding from inside its shell, and a tail with tentacles lashed out towards Meeka.

"Run Nata!"

No sooner had she said this, than one of the tentacles on a tail caught hold of Meeka's left hind leg. Meeka rose into the air, lashing out at the tentacle with her own tail, while flames shot out of her mouth.

Nata wanted to run, but her legs wouldn't move. Her feet seemed to be paralyzed. When she saw the other tail reaching out to grab her, she dropped the pouches of berries. Her feet bolted into action. Up the hill she flew, hearing the tail hit the ground with a thud just behind her. She didn't stop running until she had reached the top of the hill. Her heart pounded in her ears, and her breath came out in gasps.

So much for not needing to worry about the mere crawlers.

She looked back as she heard Meeka

shrieking and snarling. Fire spouted out of Meeka's mouth, but the tail didn't seem to be hurt by the flames. She was trying to fly into the air to break the hold of the tail, but it held onto her, dragging her closer to the water. Nata could tell that Meeka was getting tired. The tail began to drag her closer and closer. Soon the other tail would be latched onto her. If that happened, Meeka would be dragged under the water, and she would never see her again.

No.

Nata grabbed her bow and arrows, and raced down the hill. She took aim at the mere crawler's

head, and let an arrow fly. It landed in the side of its tentacle covered mouth, but it was enough to make the creature let out a deafening shriek as it let go of Meeka's leg. Meeka was up into the air just out of reach of its tails in an instant.

"Nata, look out!"

The warning came too late. One of the tails crashed down right next to her, which jolted her off her feet onto the ground. Some sort of fluid was flung from the suckers onto Nata's leg. It hurt. In fact, the pain in her leg was like nothing she had ever felt before.

"Meeka!"

The mere crawler was making a gurgling sound. The tentacles around its mouth opening and closing with a squishing noise. Nata reached down, and grabbed her knife from its sheath. She made a desperate slash at the tail, while Meeka, snarling with rage, flew at its head with her mouth spouting flames. The mere crawler's tentacle stopped pursuing Nata in order to grab Meeka, but she had already flown out of reach again.

Meeka's flames had scorched the shell black. One of the tails was rubbing at the burnt shell, while the other flailed about in the air. Nata stumbled as she picked her bow up from where it had fallen. With careful aim as she favored her leg, she let another arrow fly.

Her aim was true as the arrow embedded itself deep in between the crawler's eyes. Before she could move, Meeka flew down to grasp her in her claws even as another shriek tore through the air, and a thunderous crash sounded below them. Up to the top of the hill Meeka flew where they landed with a thud that sent Nata flying across the ground. She landed so hard that it knocked the wind out of her.

Once a dizzy spell had passed, Nata sat up, and shook her head alarmed. Meeka lay on top of the hill gasping for breath. Her leg was bleeding from the suckers of the tentacle. Nata tried to jump up to check on Meeka, but her left leg gave out from under her. She looked down to see the wound on her leg from where the tentacle sucker had sprayed her. It didn't hurt anymore, but she couldn't feel anything from her knee down. She got back up slowly, and limped over to where Meeka lay.

"Meeka, are you alright?"

Meeka gasped. "Yes."

Nata gave Meeka a dubious once over. Concerned about the amount of blood she had lost, she knelt down beside Meeka's injured leg. From her pouch of herbs, she took out some graf leaves and an ointment to cover the open wounds. Meeka was still breathing pretty hard.

"We don't have time for herbs," Meeka panted. "We must get away from here. All the noise has probably brought every mere crawler within miles. It will have to wait."

"You've lost a lot of blood. If I don't stop the bleeding now, you will be too weak to fly."

Meeka did not reply as Nata continued to place the leaves onto her open wounds. There were dozens of small circular cuts gashed into her scales. She was sure that Meeka did not realize how deep and ugly her wounds were, nor how much blood she had lost. Once Nata had the wounds covered, she gently pressed on the leaf edges to make a seal. Next, she took some of the rawhide string, and tied it around her leg to keep the leaves in place.

How did the mere crawler cut through her scales anyway? I guess the suckers on the mere crawler's tentacles must be strong as well as serrated.

Nata looked at the wound on her own leg as she washed Meeka's blood from her hands with water from her water skin.

Good thing the tentacle didn't actually manage to grab onto me, or this injury would have been a lot worse.

Her own wound did not look too bad. It was a red, raised welt, but she did not understand why her leg was numb. Then she remembered Meeka's warning about the stinging of the tentacles.

Oh.

Her tail tried to wrap around her wrist again as she gave her leg the same graf leaf treatment, using the last of the rawhide string in her pouch.

Wounds tended to, Nata looked around for the berry pouches. They were at the bottom of the hill, not too far from where the mere crawler lay with most of its body still in the water. She could just make out the fletching from her arrow that was lodged in between its eyes. Despite watching the crawler with a careful eye for a while, it never moved.

Well... dead crawler or not, I have to try to get the pouches of berries.

She picked up her spear, and, using it as a crutch, started slowly down the hill.

"Nata," Meeka croaked.

"We can't leave without the berries Meeka."

A ragged distressed noise was all that answered her as she staggered down the hill. She strained her ears for any sound, but none met her ears. The silence was eerie. All the noise must have scared away the nartals in the area, but it was the lack of noise from even the crickets that made the fur on her tail stand on end.

Keeping her eyes fixed on the crawler, Nata reached the pouches of berries she had dropped. When no further movement was forthcoming, she reached out to pick them up. The berry pouches were in her hands just as one of the tails moved. Nata froze. The tail jerked up into the air with its tentacles flared out, and waved around for a while, before it plopped down onto the ground.

Whew.

Once her heart rate was back under control, she started backing up the hill with pouches in hand. Halfway up the hill and far enough away from the mere crawler to feel safe, she turned and limped the rest of the way. Just as she reached Meeka, she could hear the now recognizable shrieking of a mere crawler in the distance.

Oh no.

—Chapter 9—

Once she reached Meeka's side at the top of the hill, Nata dropped the berry pouches on the ground next to her food pouch. Meeka's head was resting on the ground. Her mouth was open, and her sides still heaving from the exertion. Wanting to offer her some relief, Nata placed her water skin on Meeka's tongue, and let the water slowly trickle into her mouth. Meeka's eyes shone with gratitude even in her exhausted state.

While she waited for Meeka to catch her breath, Nata tied the two berry pouches together so she could drape them over Meeka's neck. Concern over the injury had her checking Meeka's wound to make sure that the bleeding had stopped. Satisfied with her diagnosis, she sat beside her dragon friend to wait. A glance up at the sky revealed dark clouds rapidly making their way across the sky in their direction.

Fabulous. Just what we need.

Well, first things first.

"Meeka, it looks like the leaves have stopped the bleeding. We can leave as soon as you feel like you can fly."

Nata didn't add that it would prudent to leave as fast as possible. She was sure that Meeka was far more aware of that than she was. Her nose would have picked up on the encroaching storm even if her eyes missed it. Fortunately, it wasn't too long before Meeka's breathing had returned to normal. She stirred, stood up while favoring her left hind leg, and flexed her wings.

"My goodness, I feel much better."

"It's not going to last long," Nata cautioned.

"In that case, get on my back, and we'll get out of here before I lose my strength."

Nata got up. The numbness in her leg had been replaced by a dull ache as she climbed on Meeka's back. Just in time too. A plopping sound came from the marsh, and the water rippled beside the dead mere crawler. Two black tentacles slipped over the body.

Oh no.

"Hang on."

With a flap of Meeka's wings, they shot up into the air. It didn't escape Nata notice that they were not flying in the direction of the colony. They were headed northwest away from the storm at least, but home was northeast. To make the situation even more dire, the storm was rapidly gaining on them.

"Where are we going?"

"The sorcerer's house."

"I thought that he wasn't going to be home for some time?"

"He isn't, but even the outside of his home will prove a safe haven considering how injured I am. I am in no shape to fly all the way back to the colony today."

Nata winced.

A glance back at the storm, revealed it to be nearly on top of them. They flew over the marsh. Its black water rippled in the wind. The stagnant odors parched her lips, and stung her nostrils. Stunted bushes and brown brush grew on small rock islands.

They had just cleared the marsh, when the wind picked up, and lightning lit up the sky followed by thunderous crashing. The storm was upon them. It wasn't long before it started raining. Just a sprinkle at first, then a steady downpour that was topped with ferocious gusts of wind.

Speed was not their ally. As the wind buffeted them, Meeka flew lower, trying to get away from the stronger wind currents. Meeka was fighting a losing battle. It was clear that the medicine she gave Meeka was wearing off. Her mouth was wide open as she gasped for breath, trying to get them to Master Pukas's house. Nata wasn't sure they were going to make it.

Just when she thought things couldn't get much worse, she started to hear that strange song again. She couldn't afford to be distracted right now. Nevertheless, it gave her something else to think about beside their current situation. The song was almost soothing, and she hummed along with it as she held on tight.

A blast of wind sent Meeka spiraling up into the air, and the song stopped. Nata almost fell off. Meeka fought to stay level while the wind pushed them along. The rain poured down, thunder boomed and lightning flashed. Just when she thought the wind would whip her right off Meeka's back, she dove down towards the ground. It took all the strength of her claws to hold on. To her dismay, when the lightning flashed again, she saw that they were not going to land on the ground.

Whyttle lake was rushing up towards them.

She had only a second to realize this before they plunged into the lake with so much force that she was knocked off Meeka's back, and into the water. Cold water washed over her, as the strong current pulled her down into the lake.

Help Meeka!

Nata lungs burned, and a warm tingle pulsed through her body. Thankfully, the current changed, and she shot upwards. She reached the surface where she started treading water, which didn't stop her from choking and sputtering.

Yuck, the water tastes like rotten romaberries.

In the next lightning flash, she saw that Meeka was swimming in front of her. Waves washed over her head as she fought to stay afloat. Nata's numb fingers caught on Meeka's horn, which she wasted no time grabbing.

Got to hang on.

She put her face against Meeka's scaly neck before she managed to pull herself back into the saddle on Meeka's back as Meeka swam towards the lakeshore. They were lucky. The shore wasn't far at all. When they reached it, Meeka slowly climbed out of the lake, limped a little way, then collapsed. Both of them were too exhausted to move.

Nata slid off. "Are you alright?"

"As well as I can be. I'm sorry. The wind was too strong for me."

"You did your best. Is there anything I can do? A drink maybe?"

"No, I've already drunk half of the lake."

It was just then that Nata realized that she'd lost everything in the lake, except her water skin and herb pouch. "I've lost the berries."

"Nothing for it right now. Come on, we must keep on going if we are ever going to get to Master Pukas's house tonight. We are going to have to get there on foot, because of my injuries and the storm."

Nata shivered. Her wet clothes clung to her as water dripped off her hair into the puddles on the ground, and her tail was a sorry sight indeed. Darkness surrounded them as Meeka placed her head on her shoulder. Her own hair tangled with Meeka's mane.

Please be all right my friend. Mama being seriously ill has been bad enough. I don't want to come that close to losing you as well.

She sighed, and patted Meeka's snout as she limped along beside her. What a bedraggled sight they must look. Elbee and dragon limping away from the lake.

I wonder how far it is to Master Pukas's house from here on foot.

It seemed like they had been walking for hours, when a grey shadow loomed up in front of them. She screamed, and grabbed Meeka, who tensed up as ready to fight as she could in her condition. But there was no need.

A soft blue light appeared, and she saw Master Pukas peering down at them from atop the blue horse with a black mane she'd seen at his home. "Well, I'm surprised to see you two again so soon, in this abominable weather that has cut my journey short no less."

Nata had never felt so relieved in her life as she stumbled over to the horse's side. "Meeka's hurt."

"What!"

Master Pukas's hair broke out in it's strange braiding again. A sight made even more peculiar than any other time she had seen it what with the storm whipping the braids, and water being flung every which way.

"She hurt her leg in a fight with a mere crawler in the marsh."

Master Pukas jumped off his horse, and raced over to Meeka. The staff he held in his hand had a blue glow of light radiating from it. She could tell he was talking to Meeka, but the noise of the storm prevented Nata from hearing what was said. Between lightning flashes, she saw him take something out of his robe that looked like a small water skin, the contents of which he poured into Meeka's mouth. Meeka coughed and sputtered while she drank it. There must have been some sort of medicine in the skin, because it wasn't long before she gave her wings a stretch, and flew up into the air.

Master Pukas watched her leave for a moment, before he headed back to his horse. "Come Nata, you will ride with me on Arrow, so that Meeka will not have the extra weight. I gave Meeka something to boost her strength for the rest of the trip."

He leaned down, gave her a boost up onto his horse, and then he climbed up behind her. She was rather glad as he tucked his robe around her, so that only the front of her face was uncovered before he started Arrow into a gallop. Rain was still coming down in sheets. Between the dunk in the lake, the rain, and the wind she was soaked to the bone. She didn't realize quite how cold she was until she was wrapped up.

Still, with Master Pukas there to look after things, she relaxed. Arrow galloped so fast that it almost took her breath away. He couldn't go as fast as Meeka of course, but Nata always loved to ride fast.

I wish Nole were here to ride with us.

Thunder boomed, lightning crackled, and the wind whipped at her face. Time seemed to pass in a daze as her exhaustion crept up on her. Before long they stopped at the front door of Master Pukas's house. It was a shame, because it let Nata know that they had almost made the flight there before Meeka's strength had given out. Still, she was just grateful that there was help at hand right now.

"Nata, go on inside where it's warm. I need to stable Arrow before I come inside. Meeka should already be there."

Sure enough, inside the house, Meeka was already lying beside the fireplace. Nata dashed over as quick as she could with her own injured leg, and knelt beside her. Meeka's eyes were closed, her mouth was open, and her breath coming out in ragged gasps again.

"Meeka?"

Nata rubbed her hands along her the mane on her neck, but she did not respond. Without a sound to announce his arrival, Master Pukas knelt down with a bowl in his hand beside her. He dipped a spoon into the liquid, and drizzled it over Meeka's tongue.

"Nata, please get me the brown mug on the shelf beside the fireplace."

She brightened, happy that there was something she could do to help even as the memory of her spilling her papa's cricket berry juice, which in turn lead to this crazy trip, haunted her. Fortunately, the mug was empty when she took it off the shelf, so at least she wouldn't have to worry about spilling something. He took the mug from her, and dipped it into the bucket of water sitting beside him. With gentle hands, he lifted Meeka's chin, then poured the water from the mug into her mouth. In no time at all, Meeka's breathing had eased as she fell into a deep slumber.

"How exactly was she wounded, and what did you treat the wound with?"

"Meeka was grabbed by one of the tentacles on one of the tails. The other wounds would just be bruises and strained muscles from the struggle. I am quite certain that her wings were wrenched in the whole debacle as well. I put an ointment for open wounds on her left hind leg, and used the graf leaves with a sealing paste to help prevent further blood loss."

Master Pukas exhaled slowly. "Very well. I trust your treatment knowledge as I saw your capability when I check your own injury last time you were here. It's best to let such wounds rest to prevent infection, so I will wait until morning to remove the leaves. What of your own injuries?"

Nata yawned as she had trouble keeping her eyes open. "Pretty much the same, only I just got caught by something sprayed from the suckers on the tentacle instead of grabbed."

He nodded. "Time for sleep then. Take my bed for the night. I will watch after Meeka."

She limped over towards the bed, and stumbled. Master Pukas reached down to catch her just before she fell onto the floor. He picked her up in his arms, gently placed her in bed, and tucked the blanket around her.

"Dragon guard your dreams Nata."

Trees shield you from sight," Nata mumbled.

She woke to the loudest snoring sounds she had ever heard. Master Pukas was sitting in the chair beside the fireplace with his head resting on the back of the chair, mouth open, and snoring. She started to giggle, but stopped as memories of yesterday flooded her mind. When she glanced over at Meeka, she could see her still lying on the floor beside the fireplace fast asleep with her stomach moving up and down as she breathed. Nata quietly climbed out of bed, and crept over to where Meeka was lying. The ache from her injury yesterday seemed to be gone, which was a great relief to her mind.

Just a peek is all she wanted.

Master Pukas let out an explosive snort as he woke up. "Awake at last I see. I stayed up the rest of the night to make sure neither of you had any ill effects from your encounter, and I was beginning to think that you would sleep the day away."

Nata blushed. "Sorry."

"Nothing to be sorry about. I expected as much after your adventures yesterday."

Nata's stomach rumbled.

"Ah, hungry are you? It was around noon when I last had a bite to eat, and it looks to be a few hours since then. I must have fallen asleep after the meal. How are you feeling?"

"Better than I was last night."

"Good, good. Let's have a something to eat before we have a look at Meeka's leg."

Nata moved over to the table as Master Pukas gathered some fish, and placed them in two bowls. From there he went over to the shelf beside the fireplace, and took down the big brown jar. Out of the jar came four corn muffins as well as some cheese. He sliced off two pieces of cheese, and placed them in the bowls with a couple of corn muffins and the fish.

As he reached the table, he handed her one of the bowls. "Here we are. Eat up."

Where in Aquatia did Master Pukas get corn muffins!?

The meal was a delicious, but there was something familiar about the corn muffins. They tasted a lot like the ones that Mrs. Simo cooked.

Does Mrs. Simo make corn muffins for Master Pukas too?

She didn't get the chance to ask. Just as they finished eating, Meeka's claw moved, and she opened one lavender eye.

Nata felt the tension ease out of her shoulders. "Day greet you! How are you feeling?"

Meeka grimaced. "Tired and sore."

Master Pukas hummed as he headed over to Meeka's side. "That's to be expected. Come Nata, it is time to unwrap Meeka's leg."

Nata sat the bowl she had just finished eating out of down by the fireplace. "Okay."

"Now, let's see how bad your leg is. A mere crawler's tentacle usually leaves a nasty set of wounds." It didn't take him long to have everything set up, and he was soon cutting off the rawhide strings before he peeled back the graf leaves.

—Chapter 10—

Wwhen Master Pukas finished removing the graf leaves, he sucked in a sharp breath.

Nata tried to look over Master Pukas's shoulder. "What is it? Is something wrong?"

Meeka attempted to crane her neck around to look. "Are the wounds that bad?"

Master Pukas shook his head. "There are no wounds. Not even any scars in her scales."

"But...," Nata chewed on her lip. "I don't understand. When I placed the leaves on Meeka's leg, there were several circular wounds. How could the wounds have healed so quickly?"

Meeka nodded. "The pain was almost unbearable before it went numb."

"I believe you, but your leg is completely healed today." There was an odd spark in his eyes, a mix of both hope and dread, as Master Pukas turned his gaze on Nata. "Are you *sure* you told me everything you did to patch up Meeka's leg yesterday?"

Nata swallowed hard as her tail wrapped around her waist. "Yes. All I did was put some ointment on the wounds, and seal them with some graf leaves."

Master Pukas rubbed his chin with his hand. "Well, this is interesting. Very interesting indeed."

Meeka and Nata stared at Master Pukas in bafflement.

"Yes, very interesting indeed," he mused.

He turned the leaves over in his hand, looked closely at them, and then at Meeka's leg. "Nata, how is your leg doing?"

Looking down at it, she remembered that it no longer bothered her when she woke up. "It doesn't hurt."

Master Pukas came over to look at it. "Let me see."

Nata lifted her leg. "Meeka distracted the mere crawler before it could latch onto me. I don't think it was very bad."

He removed the graf leaf from her leg, and she was astonished to see that welt was gone. Not only was the welt gone, but there wasn't a mark on her leg at all.

"What in Aquatia?" she spluttered.

"Hmm..., perhaps—" Master Pukas's eyes were intent as they focused on her. "Nata, have you ever been told the story of Shea'a?"

Nata blinked. "Yes, Papa used to tell me the story every night before I went to bed. But I thought it was only a bedtime story."

Maybe I'll get some answers about Shea'a now.

"Oh, it's not just a story though I have not seen tail nor fur of my dear friend for quite some time."

"But... I thought you and your sister were the only sorcerer's that had ever existed."

"Mmm, no that would be incorrect. Once there were a great many, but that's a tale for another time. What is important is the fact that there are different types of sorcerers. I am what is referred to as a caster, while my sister is an enhancer. Shea'a is a healer type."

"Is?" Meeka questioned.

Wow, just how old is Master Pukas anyway?

Master Pukas turned to look at Meeka. "Yes, is. I have yet to have conclusive evidence of her death, and I shall believe she yet lives until I have such evidence."

Meeka was solemn as she nodded. "I would do the same."

"Anyway," Master Pukas turned back to look at Nata, "while you are descendant in a long line of healers, you have not utilized magic to do so. Instead, you rely upon the world around you to provide medicines to heal with."

"But...," Nata frowned, "if I did somehow manage to heal with magic, how could it have happened?"

"I'm not sure," Master Pukas muttered. "You would have to have a catalyst, and I will hold out hope that Shea'a still lives."

Meeka cocked her head to one side. "Catalyst?"

What does Shea'a still being alive or not have to do with anything?

"A catalyst is used to awaken magic in the user," he sighed. "But assuming that Shea'a is still alive..."

Meeka huffed. "Whether by magic or herbs, I am grateful my leg is healed."

I wonder if those purple stones Meeka and I found are the catalyst that Master Pukas keeps referring to?

"Do you really think that I used magic?" Nata asked in a whisper as her shock over the whole situation began to abate.

"I can't see any other logical alternative at the moment." Masker Pukas replied.

Nata's eyes lit up.

Maybe I will be able to heal Mama with magic, and not need the berries then!

Master Pukas's eyes narrowed. "We can figure out what your catalyst is later. Regardless, you shouldn't be doing any magic for some time, especially after doing a healing this big."

"But—"

"Magic takes a lot out of you," he chided. "You might feel okay now, but I doubt Nami and Nomo would be happy if you keeled over trying to use healing magic."

Nata sighed as she hunched down in her seat. "Yes, Master Pukas."

He chuckled. "Don't be too disappointed. It takes some time to build up magic reserves. Usually a healer starts out fixing cuts and bruises."

Nata closed her eyes.

Well, with magic out, I guess that leaves going back to those abominable marshes to get more cricket berries.

"I lost everything when we plunged into the lake, so I will need to at least go get some more cricket berries." Nata mused before she opened her eyes, and focused on Master Pukas. "Unless you have some?"

Master Pukas's eyes twinkled. "Ah, I have some good news I believe. I went searching, close to the lake where I found you this morning, after I was certain that it would be safe to leave you two for a bit. I found your sealed pouches, some of which held plenty of cricket berries, beside the lake.

"Oh thank the suns!" Nata gasped. "That's a relief. Thank you Master Pukas."

He smiled. "Think nothing of it. I am afraid I took the liberty of removing the corn muffins from your pouch for us to eat. The rest of your things that I found are hanging up by the well to dry."

"Is Meeka going to be able to fly us home today?"

"No," Master Pukas gave her a frustrated glare, "and this time please do not take off without so much as a by your leave okay? It's late, and neither of you are in any condition for the trip back to the colony even if you could make it before nightfall."

Nata blushed before she nodded.

He gave Meeka and Nata both a suspicious glare before he seemed to read their intent to remain, and relaxed. "If that's settled, I need to go check up on something. Nata, since you seem to want something to do, how would you like to feed and brush Arrow?"

Nata's eyes lit up. "Could I?"

He smiled. "Certainly."

"Well, I'm hungry." Meeka grumbled. "Unless it's going to cause a problem, I'm going to go catch some fish to eat."

Master Pukas nodded. "You should be fine. In fact, that might be the best thing for you right now."

Meeka perked up. "That's the best news I've heard today."

Nata giggled as Meeka hurried out of the house, licking her chops as she left, and muttering about fish. Master Pukas and Nata followed Meeka outside, and headed out to the wooden barn beside his house where Arrow slept. After Master Pukas had finished giving her instructions, he left her alone with Arrow.

Nata smiled. "Hi Arrow, my name is Nata. You're a beautiful horse aren't you?"

He whinnied and bobbed his head.

She laughed. "Well, glad to see that you agree with me."

The first thing she did was fill Arrow's water bowl with fresh water, and then she started to put food into his food bowl. While he ate, Nata brushed his blue coat. He didn't seem to mind this, but his blue eyes kept glancing at her from time to time.

Combing the mats out of Arrow's black mane took a while, but he seemed to enjoy the attention.

"I really don't know what to think of this healing magic that Master Pukas thinks I have. I mean me?"

—Chapter 11—

*A*rrow nuzzled her hand. He must have felt she needed the support, because every once in a while he would nuzzle her hand again. Taking care of Arrow was relaxing, and she felt her cares melt away. However, all good things come to an end, and she was soon out of things to do. When she left, Arrow whinnied, stomped his feet, and snorted as if trying to say thank you.

Nata giggled. "You're welcome."

Meeka was beside the lake gobbling green gobin fish when she walked out the barn.

Nata strolled over to join Meeka by the

lakeside as she ate. "Not hungry anymore?"

"Nope, best fish I've ever tasted," Meeka smacked her teeth together.

Nata laughed. "Well then, if they are so good, do you think you could you catch me a couple to cook for supper?"

Meeka sniffed. "Yes, I suppose I could."

A few dips in the water later, and Meeka had caught her two good-sized fish. Rather than take them inside to clean them, Nata sat by the lakeside with Meeka while she got the fish ready to cook.

Meeka sighed when she finished, and got ready to head inside. "I miss Papa's cooked fish."

Nata slumped. "Me too. When Mama gets better, we'll have to convince him to make some. Hopefully, before Mama gets stir crazy enough to try cooking again."

Meeka and Nata both had matching pained expressions on their faces at that.

Mama might be a great hunter, but a good cook she was not.

She patted Meeka's side before she grabbed the fish, and headed inside. It was a good thing Master Pukas had all his cooking supplies near the fire. She might have trouble figuring out what was meant for food, and what was meant for something else in the mess his home was. Once she had the fish started, she looked around the house.

Well, I did think this place could use a good cleaning. Now's as good a time as any.

The table seemed a good place to start, so she cleaned the cobwebs off of the table legs and swept the floor. Next, she started to straighten the top of the table. There were books stacked up all over the place that she placed on the empty shelf beside the table. At the bottom of the stack she came across the strange book with the dragon on it.

Hmm..., Master Pukas said I could use magic now. Perhaps he wouldn't mind if I took just a little peek?

Just as she looked at the dragon on the cover, the eyes seemed to glow. Nata jerked, and almost dropped the book before she put the book back on the table.

Maybe it was just the light?

She kept glancing at the book as she straightened the table, afraid that she might have woken something up she shouldn't have. A faint buzzing sounded in her ears again. It seemed like the book was drawing her to it, asking her to open it.

Just a quick peek inside.

She picked up the book again, and started to open it. Just then a loud banging noise from outside startled her, and she dropped the book on the floor. The noise also stopped the buzzing in her ears.

My goodness, didn't Master Pukas tell me to leave that book alone. What was I thinking?

Nata rubbed her eyes, picked up the book, and placed it on the table. Her nose chose that moment to remind her to check on the fish. A burnt dinner after the past few days would be awful. Nata shuddered. The first meal she had at Master Pukas's house was bad enough. She had no desire for a repeat anytime soon. The front door opened with a creak just as she was taking the fish off the fire.

"Something sure smells good," Master Pukas commented as he came in the house with Meeka at his heels.

"Thanks, Meeka caught us some fish for dinner," she put the now cooked fish in the bowls on the table before she took the last four corn muffins out of the jar, and placed two in each bowl.

Master Pukas grinned. "Generous of her."

Meeka sniffed. "I am the very soul of generosity."

Nata giggled while Master Pukas covered his grin with his hand. Once he got his chuckles under control, he placed two pina fruits beside the bowls along with two mugs of cider. Master Pukas sat on his chair at the table, while Nata opted to sit beside Meeka near the fireplace on the stone floor.

"Well," Master Pukas rubbed his fingers along his long pointed nose, "something has stirred up the mountain dragons. Tomorrow, I think you and Meeka need to start flying home just before it starts to get light. Hopefully, you will both be rested enough."

"What do you think is going on?" Nata murmured between bites of food.

He shrugged. "I'm not really sure yet."

"The forest feels alive tonight," Meeka commented.

Master Pukas chuckled. "You are quite right. It would be safe to say that staying inside the house tonight is a very good idea. I wish I had some ammera flowers. They are exceptionally good at deterring visitors. I tried to grow them here for protection and medicine once, but they wouldn't take root."

Meeka sniffed. "Thank goodness for small mercies. But, as much as I detest those awful smelly flowers, I wouldn't mind if we had one to drive away unwanted visitors right now."

Master Pukas and Nata both laughed at Meeka, which caused her to do a lot of sniffing. Dinner was over all too soon, and it was time for sleep.

Meeka walked over to the corner, and laid down. "Time for bed Nata. The hours before daylight will come sooner than you would wish."

With a sigh of contentment, she closed her eyes, and went to sleep.

Master Pukas barred the front door, and stoked up the fire before he curled up in his bed for the night. "She's right. I need to get an early start as well."

Nata nodded. "Okay."

"Dragon guard your dreams Nata," he whispered.

"Trees shield you from sight," she replied.

Before she went to bed, she washed up her bowl, then she laid down next to Meeka, and wrapped a blanket around her legs. She wondered if she would sleep after having slept so late into the day. As she lay there listening to Meeka and Master Pukas snoring, she heard a weird squishing and clicking sound outside.

Did... did a mere crawler follow us all the way here?

No. No that's not possible.

Isn't it?

She shuddered.

I'm glad Master Pukas and Meeka are here... I wish Mama, Papa, or Nole were here too.

Got to get some sleep.

It seemed like a minute had passed when Master Pukas woke her before the suns were up. "Nata, there's a mug of cider, some bread, and cheese on the table for you. When you finish eating, please come outside. Meeka and I will be waiting for you."

Nata blinked at him with bleary eyes. "Okay."

"Don't forget to pick up your things on the way out." Master Pukas grunted as he walked out the front door.

Guess he's not a morning person.

Nata's mind was still clouded with sleep, but she managed to eat the bread and cheese on the table before washing it down with some cider. She even managed to pick up her travel pouch and the berry pouches as she walked outside.

"Be careful on your way home you two."

Meeka nodded. "Just to be safe, I plan to fly towards Drall Mounds, and take the long way home."

I hope we get home okay. All this excitement lately is wearing me out.

"Nata, tell Nomo I'll stop in to see him soon. I would really rather accompany you both home, but Arrow would not be able to keep up with a dragon. I won't be too long, but I have plans to stop in to talk to my sister, Megg, on the way to the colony."

Nata covered a wide yawn with her hand. "Okay Master Pukas."

He glanced closely at Nata with his eyebrows furrowed in thought for just a second. "Safe winds."

"Dragon keep you," she responded.

Master Pukas climbed up onto Arrow, and

galloped off. Once he was out of sight, Meeka flew up into the air with her wings flapping furiously in the direction of home.

Yes, there is a tense feeling in the air. A watching and waiting as if something is about to happen. What was Master Pukas worried about I wonder?

It was still dark, so she couldn't see anything yet, but she could listen. She needed to stay alert for possible signs of danger. For some reason, she felt exhausted and had to fight to stay awake. In fact, it was becoming harder and harder to stay awake. Nata wanted to tell Meeka, but a fog was taking over her mind. Vaguely, she remembered reaching the other side of the lake, and passing Drall Mounds. The sky started to get light with the promise of a new day.

Normally, the birds were awake and up in the sky with the first light of day. Today the birds and birdcalls were few and far between. As her foggy mind was trying to puzzle out this thought, she began to doze off.

Out of nowhere Meeka spoke, jerking her awake, and just in time too. "Nata, a mountain dragon was here recently. I can still smell him, and there is another smell in the air. One that I have never smelled before."

"What do you think it is?"

"I have no idea. Best keep a sharp eye out."

"Will do."

They flew for a while longer before Meeka glanced over her shoulder to see Nata's eyes closing in sleep. "Nata! You must stay awake."

"Sorry Meeka, I'm... just s... o ti... red..."

Suddenly, Nata was floating. She floated through puffs of white clouds in the blue sky. A peculiar whistling sound was singing in her ear.

It seemed like a dark shadow was reaching out to crush her.

So much wind...

Wind...

—Chapter 12—

Cool wind whipped around her face. Her braided green hair drummed a staccato rhythm into her back. There was nothing but green stretched out before her eyes. It took her a moment to realize that the green was a sea of green grass that was waving in the wind.

Meeka caught Nata in her claws, inches above the grasses.

The next time Nata opened her bleary eyes, she was lying on her back on the grass with Meeka's eyes peering down into her own with a worried expression on her face. "Mee... ka?"

"Oh thank the suns, do you remember what

happened?"

"There was… a dark shadow after me."

Meeka shook her head. "You went to sleep, and slid off of my back. I was lucky I was quick enough to catch you. Perhaps we should have stayed at Master Pukas's house today."

"I'm sorry Meeka. I don't know what's wrong with me. I know Master Pukas said that magic takes a lot out of you, but I felt fine yesterday. Right now, I've never felt so tired and weak."

"Well, it's too dangerous for us to be sitting out here in the open. We'd better think of something quick. We are closer to home than Drall Mounds."

"Maybe if I walk a little, it will help me wake up?"

"I don't think that is a good idea. There is nowhere to hide here, and the trees offer little protection."

Nata tried in vain to keep her eyes open.

Well… this is a fine kettle of fish.

"Do you still have a rope in your pouch, or did you lose it?"

Puzzled, she looked at Meeka. "What do you want with a rope?"

"You can use the rope to tie yourself to the saddle. That way, if you fall asleep, you will not fall off."

All around them, the noise of birds and

animal had ceased.

"Hurry," Meeka whispered.

Nata pulled out some rope as soon as she had climbed back up on Meeka's back, and began tying herself to the saddle.

"Make sure the knots are tight."

"Okay," Nata yawned. "Ready to go."

Meeka quickly flew up into the air, flying as fast as she safely could for home. Nata didn't remember much of their flight home, for she soon fell asleep.

Nata woke up the next morning quite surprised at finding herself in her own bed. She glanced around the room with her gaze coming to rest on her mama, who was sleeping.

I hope she is feeling better.

Must have fallen asleep again after I climbed onto Meeka's back yesterday. It's a good thing Meeka had me tie myself onto her.

Nata climbed out of bed, and tiptoed across the room to the table.

There she found a hunk of cheese, and some freshly baked bread. She looked over at Mama as she sighed, and turned over in her sleep.

Papa and Meeka must be gone.

It was quiet. Too quiet in the colony today. It gave her an eerie feeling, which caused a chill to run up and down her spine. She ate some corn crackers, fish, and pina fruit. Satisfied, she tiptoed out of the room to look for Papa and Meeka. She walked through Meeka's lair, to the deck outside, and bumped into Master Pukas.

"Oh!" For some reason it felt like he towered over her.

"Well, I see you have finally gotten up. Are you feeling better today?"

"I think so."

He was looking down into her face so intently that she found herself looking away.

"Yes, well, that remains to be seen. Your eyes do appear to be clearer than they were yesterday. It seems that I should have looked a little more carefully into things before you left. From what Meeka has told me, you nearly met with a disaster.

Nata blushed.

"But I have something I want to look into today that could possibly use your help. Pack yourself something to eat please as we might be gone quite a while."

"Okay Master Pukas."

Nata was quite astonished and puzzled as she went into the house to pack a food pouch.

I wonder what in Aquatia he thinks I can help him with?

She took the herb pouch off her belt to put some graf leaves in it. When she opened the pouch, she noticed that the purple stones were faintly glowing.

Oh no! In all the excitement, I forgot to tell Papa about them... or Master Pukas...

These stones are rather conspicuous, and I can't think of anything else I might have picked up that might be a catalyst.

I hope I'll have a chance to ask today.

She finished grabbing some supplies for a day trip as well as her ever faithful knife, and walked out onto the deck. Master Pukas was already down on the ground, standing beside Arrow, so she climbed down the ladder to join him.

"Master Pukas, does Papa know I am going to be with you today?"

"Yes."

"What about Mama? Is it safe to leave her alone?"

"Nami will be fine. We had quite a long talk together before you got up this morning. As annoyed as she was by the prospect of yet more rest, she decided to lie back down."

Master Pukas lifted her up onto Arrow's back, climbed up behind her, and off they went.

It was a cloudy day. The threat of rain was hanging heavily in the air. Arrow was weaving a path through the forest. The sunlight danced off his blue coat and black mane.

Stunted, yellow-leaf opsan trees dotted their path, while huge elban trees filled the sky above them. The elban trees were a unique chameleon like tree. Nobody was exactly sure what governed the change in the elban trees. Sometimes it seemed to be affected by the weather, at other times it seemed to be the change in the seasons. Today the trees had sliver-green barked branches, and blue leaves with purple highlights running through them.

A fragrant smell teased her nose, and Nata flinched as she closed her eyes. It took her a moment to blink away the tears as she breathed in the scent of the pink nally bush flowers.

Why do those accursed flowers have to smell so nice. This whole mess began with them anyway.

Nata could still remember the fright she felt when Mama had gotten poisoned by the nally bush. The thorns were quite poisonous, and problematic to work around. Unfortunately, the flowers of the nally bush were an important herbal remedy. Nata had been learning how to gather the flowers by watching Mama harvest them from the bush, when a stampede of wild lefrodels came charging through the clearing. Mama had managed to push her out of the way, but was pushed into the nally bush and poisoned by the thorns. Nata was exceedingly grateful that Meeka was there to rush them back home to Papa, or Mama might not have survived.

Learning to be a healer was dangerous work.

As they galloped along the forest, they occasionally saw clumps of yellow fern and purple moss-covered rocks. They followed a narrow stream that had green lepas pads floating on the water's surface. The aroma from their yellow flowers filled the air.

They came into a small clearing, where a hut was well hidden from the sky by the trees that overshadowed it. Arrow stopped in front of the door, and Master Pukas climbed down.

"Here we are."

Nata followed Master Pukas as he went into the hut. She was still extremely confused about what was going on. The hut was similar to the homes in the colony, but instead of being in a tree it was built on the ground. To be honest, with the hut being on the ground instead of the trees, it reminded her of Master Pukas's house.

"Master Pukas, whose home is this?"

"This is Shea'a's home. She used to live here while working on perfecting her spells. Although it has been a long time since I have seen her, and I have looked here before, I wanted to have another look for clues to where she may have gone. Since you seem to be able to use healing magic, I was hoping we might find something new here."

"How come?"

I wonder if this would be a good time to mention the stones Meeka and I found.

"Sometimes magic traces are dependent on the type of magic used."

Nata's green eyes were round as saucers as she looked up at him. "But I don't understand—"

"That's all I'll say for now, help me look for anything out of the ordinary please."

Nata shrugged. "Okay."

Guess not.

Together, they started to search through the hut. Master Pukas used his staff to tap around the stone fireplace, looked up the chimney, and tapped along the walls. He picked up the firewood stacked beside the fireplace one piece at a time. There must have been nothing there either, because he sighed as he stacked it back beside the fireplace.

Nata picked up jars and pots, turning them upside down, looking everywhere. She even took the broom beside the door, and started to sweep the cobwebs off the ceiling. There was so much dust, she started sweeping it out the door. All of the dust caused both of them to do a lot of sneezing.

Master Pukas must have decided he had enough inside as sneezed his way outside, and started looking around on the ground beside the hut. Nata had just walked outside to join him, when a faint buzzing sound started in her ears. She must have had a strange look on her face, for Master Pukas stopped beside her.

"Nata, is something wrong?"

"No."

The blue frogs croaked as she looked up at the sky. It had grown dark with storm clouds, and she knew it was going to rain soon. Nata gave a little shudder, and started to look around on the ground using a stick to turn over rocks. Master Pukas was standing not too far from her, intently watching everything she did.

"Mmm," he mused.

The buzzing sound was growing in her ears, and she rubbed them as she glanced at the sky. "Master Pukas, I feel like there is something in the sky looking for me."

Nata backed up until she stood beside him, all the while looking up into the sky. Even Arrow could sense something, for he snorted and stomped his feet.

Master Pukas patted his neck. "Whoa, boy. It's okay."

That seemed to calm him some. Arrow stopped snorting, and just stood there with his head and ears up. It started to drizzle, and she could hear thunder claps getting closer.

"Nata, go inside the hut, and wait for me please."

Nata nodded. She wondered what Master Pukas was going to do. The sky suddenly opened up with rain as she dashed inside. Lightning flashed and thunder boomed. It wasn't long before he came back. They stood together inside the hut, and watched the rain pour down. The buzzing sound in her ears had ceased when the rain started.

"Quite a storm," Master Pukas shouted. "I managed to find some shelter for Arrow."

It rained for a while before it tapered off, but the sky remained cloudy.

Master Pukas cleared his throat. "Now that you can hear without having to shout, there is something that I would like to know. What made you think there was something in the sky looking for you?"

"I don't know. I just sort of got this feeling…"

"Anything specific? Or why you were rubbing your ears?"

"My ears? Oh, a faint buzzing sound started in my ears when I came outside after we had searched the hut. It never went away. The buzzing just kept getting louder, and I had this strange feeling that something was up in the sky looking for me."

"Mmm, I see. Have you ever heard this buzzing sound in your ears before today?"

"Yes, I was going to tell Papa, but I forgot. Do you know what is causing it?"

Master Pukas went over to the fireplace and put some wood on it. He took his staff, struck the wood, and started a fire. She hadn't even realized how chilly it had become since it had rained though she could hear the remnants of water droplets from the storm dripping from leaves in the forest.

"Come Nata, sit down please."

Nata crossed the room, and sat on stool beside the fireplace. Looking at Master Pukas now, she could see the hints of some hidden dread as if he suspected something that he wished was not true.

He clasped his hands in his lap as he joined her in sitting in front of the fireplace. "It seems we need to talk, and we might as well be warm. Try to start at the beginning, and tell me when you first heard the buzzing in your ears."

Maybe now I will find out if those stones truly are the catalyst that Master Pukas was talking about.

Nata took a deep breath. "The first time I heard the buzzing was after I left your house with the ammera flower. Meeka and I had just flown across the lake when it started. She took us to the Drall Mounds, but it wasn't just a buzzing sound then. It was more like a song. The second time I heard just the song, and it was during the storm when Meeka and I were leaving the Mere Marshes. The third time it happened was when I was cleaning your house, and found that book with the dragon on it. The fourth and last time it happened was on our trip home yesterday."

"Is that all that happened? Just singing?"

"Well, no, a very strange thing happened while we were inside Drall Mounds. When I took my pouch off my belt and opened it, the two stones that we found were glowing with a purple fire."

"Do you have them with you?"

"Yes, they're right here." Nata opened her herb pouch, and took out the stones. They were glowing faintly with a purple light.

He closed his eyes, and his whole body, tail and all, seemed to droop. "Where did you find them?"

Nata hesitated before she answered. "We found them in the sand on our way home from getting the ammera flower."

"I see," he muttered. "So this is the trifle Meeka stopped to look at."

Does this mean they aren't a catalyst?

"Nata, hold your hands out, so that I can have a look at them."

It looked like he had wrapped his own hands in a blue light, when he reached out toward the stones.

To her shock, they burst into flames.

"What—"

—Chapter 13—

*N*ata jumped. She would have dropped the stones, but Master Pukas steadied her hands.

"Hold still Nata. Whatever you do, don't drop them!"

Is this what he meant by a catalyst?

"What's going on?"

"This... is an awakening. I've only ever seen Megg and I's awakening. Shea'a was awakened before the two of us."

It took her a moment to process the fact that the fire didn't actually feel like it was burning her. In fact, the fire was actually soothing. The purple

125

fire crept up her arms, and, in no time at all, enveloped her entire form. That strange melody that she had been hearing was back, growing stronger than ever until it reached a crescendo. The fire felt like warmth and safety with the song echoing serenity. Gradually, the glow of the fire died down, and the song faded away.

She felt different, revitalized, as if she had been straining to reach something, and finally succeeded. Then she caught sight of her hair.

"What happened to my hair!?" Nata yelped as she pulled her braid around her neck.

Her previously green hair was now as pure white as snow.

Wait, what about my tail?

She twisted her tail around in front of her so she could see, and, sure enough, the fur on her tail was as white as her hair.

"Ah, I forgot to mention that." Master Pukas chuckled. "That is the mark of a sorcerer or sorceress you see."

"A little warning would've been nice."

Master Pukas's eyes twinkled even though his face looked sad. "It's not so bad. You look quite elegant."

The fire had faded from the stones in her hands, which made them look deceptively innocent. "So these were a catalyst?"

"Yes, go ahead and put the stones away. With the change in your hair, it will be impossible to hide that you are now a sorceress, but, for now, let's try to keep what catalyst you had known to a limited number of people."

"Why, are they special in some way?"

"Yes, but we'll discuss that later. I don't want to overwhelm you with too much information at once."

"Okay," Nata sighed as she put the stones back into her pouch.

She wasn't at all sure she was ready to be a magic healer or any healer just yet. What was Nole going to say when I tell him? Am I going to have to leave Mama and Papa, and live in this hut.

Master Pukas seemed to read her thoughts as she glanced around the hut.

He chuckled. "Come Nata, I don't think you will have to live in this hut."

Nata ducked her head behind her tail as she blushed.

"I should have asked you more questions when you healed Meeka's leg. It would have saved me a lot of searching."

Nata opened her mouth to apologize, but Master Pukas shook his head. "Perhaps you should have mentioned the stones earlier, but the fault ultimately lies with me. You have no experience with magic, and could not have known. Never forget that Nata. I may be your elder and more experienced, but I am just as prone to making mistakes as anyone else. My apologies for putting you in unnecessary danger."

Nata's eyes were wide as she nodded. "Accepted."

Master Pukas opened the door to the hut. "Come on then, let us return to your home."

The two of them went round to where Arrow was stabled under some shelter from the storm. Rain water still dripped off the leaves of trees, and the ground was soaked. Before long they were on Arrow's back traveling towards the colony.

Nata felt a grin cross her face despite the massive upheaval in her life.

Riding on Arrow was not quite as fun as Meeka, but fairly close all the same.

With growing amazement, she watched him pick a path through the sodden forest. His black hooves skimmed the forest floor, while his ears twitched back and forth. Brown furry monkeys, chattered in the trees above them. He slowed to a trot, but still managed to skirt around bushes and trees that had loomed up in front of their path.

Master Pukas seemed deep in thought, so she remained silent for the rest of the ride home. Once back at the colony, Master Pukas and Nata dismounted. Arrow shook his head as he trotted off towards the water trough. They climbed up the ladder to her house, and were greeted by Meeka, Papa, and Mama.

"Master Pukas! Nata!" Mama exclaimed.

Nata ran over and hugged her. "Mama! You're up!"

Mama laughed. "Yes. A few more days of rest, and I'll be just fine. But what on Aquatia happened to your hair?"

Nata blinked before glancing at Master Pukas. "Oh—er…"

Master Pukas interrupted. "That's a discussion best held inside."

Mama and Papa glanced at each other before they nodded, and started heading inside. Master Pukas and Nata followed close behind with Meeka bringing up the rear.

They all found some comfortable places to sit, or in Meeka's case lay, before Master Pukas began. "My earlier suspicions that I discussed with you before we left, turned out to be correct. Nata has indeed awakened as a sorceress. The change in her hair color is a result of the awakening completing."

"Oh…, is that why your hair is white Master Pukas," Mama blushed. "I thought it was just because you were old."

Master Pukas gave Mama an exasperated look. "Thanks Nami."

Mama's expression was positively impish as

she replied. "You're welcome."

Nata giggled.

Master Pukas shook his head even as his lips twitched in mirth. Nata was glad. He had been so solemn lately. It was good to see him smile.

Master Pukas looked at Mama and Papa. "At any rate she is a healer type sorceress like Shea'a."

Papa had a proud look on his face. "Truly?"

"Yes," Master Pukas replied. "Nata, show them your catalyst."

Nata took the purple stones out of her pouch, and held them up so everyone could see them. The stones gave off a faint glow of purple light. Papa, Mama, and Meeka all gazed at the glowing stones in awe.

"Nata," Mama breathed. "Where did you find those?"

"Well," Nata began. "Meeka and I found them in the Sand Desert on our way back from getting the ammera flower. We saw something sparkling in the sand, investigated, and found the stones."

"Yes, the trifle in the sand," Master Pukas chuckled.

Meeka sniffed indignantly. "Who would have thought those plain little stones would end up being a catalyst?"

They laughed, because they knew that dragons loved finding treasure.

Mama looked at Master Pukas. "What does it all mean?"

"Well," Master Pukas muttered. "I am not entirely sure. There are a lot of things that we do not know yet. Why were the stones found now? What happened to Shea'a?"

Nata twiddled her fingers. "Do... you think Shea'a is dead?"

Master Pukas fixed Nata with a hard stare. "Why do you say that?"

"Well," Nata gulped, "I remember you mentioning something about Shea'a still being alive when we were talking about catalysts, and then you seemed so sad when I brought the stones out."

Master Pukas sighed. "A good memory you have there. I suppose this is a good time for a small lesson on magic users. You remember I said that there are different types of magic users?"

Nata nodded.

Master Pukas stroked his goatee. "There are four different types of magic users."

Nata tilted her head to the side. "You mentioned three before: healer, caster, and enhancer."

Master Pukas smiled. "That's right. The fourth type is the enchanter. Another rule of magic is that there are never any more or less users of magic at any one point in time, and a catalyst can only belong to one person at a time as well."

Nata blinked. "Huh?"

"For example," Master Pukas cleared his throat. "This catalyst previously belonged to Shea'a. They could only have been used to awaken magic in another user if Shea'a was dead, and a new user had inherited her magic. A catalyst can be destroyed, but, if it isn't, then it is easy to track who the newest person inherited magic from."

Nata frowned. "But... I thought you said there were many magic users at one time. If there are always the same amount of magic users, where are all of the others?"

Master Pukas drooped. "For the moment, I'd like to stick to the basics, and that's a long story we'll get into another time."

"Okay," Nata chewed on her lip. "How come I inherited the magic and when? Was I born with it?"

Master Pukas shook his head. "Not necessarily, it could have been when you were born, or later. Magic can choose it's next barer at any point in their life."

Nata's eyes were wide as saucers. "You mean magic is alive?"

"In a way." Master Pukas nodded. "It isn't a proven fact yet, at least as far as we know, but the way magic chooses it's next barer does at least seem to indicate some sort of sentience."

"Oh," Nata's tail wrapped around her wrist.

"So the fact that I have Shea'a's catalyst means she is gone?"

Master Pukas sighed. "Yes."

"Oh...," Nata mumbled. "I'm sorry for your loss."

Master Pukas smiled sadly. "Thank you. I believe Megg and I suspected, but we hoped it wasn't true. Regardless, I am going to go speak with my sister tomorrow. Sometime later, I want to take Nata back to the place where she found the stones, if Meeka can find it, to see if there is anything else there. Nata, please remember to keep the stones secret for now."

Nata nodded. "I will."

"Well," Mama clapped her hands before she got a sleeping mat out of the big chest, and spread it in front of the fireplace for Master Pukas. "It's late. Let's all grab a bite to eat, and head to bed."

"Yes, Mama," Papa replied.

Before long everyone was fed, and heading towards their beds for the night.

Mama tucked Nata into bed. "Dragon guard your dreams."

"Trees shield you from sight." Nata mumbled with bleary eyes.

Master Pukas was gone the next morning when Nata woke up. She was distracted from wondering what he went to discuss with his sister by the return of the hunters. The whole village was excited. As with every time the hunters came back successful, there was to be a big feast with lots of music and dancing to celebrate.

—Chapter 14—

ata was anxious to see Nole, but Mama kept her busy peeling and slicing the pina fruits for the celebration. She was just about to burst, when Papa returned to say it was time to get ready. He had been helping the hunters cook the meat for the feast. They had returned with enough meat to last through most of the winter.

It's seems like it's been forever since I've seen Nole. I wonder what he is going to think of the whole sorceress thing.

Nata dressed in her celebration clothes before she braided and beaded her hair.

Mama grinned. "Let me look at you."

She danced over to Mama before she spun around so she could see her.

Mama laughed, and her green eyes sparkled. "Papa, I think our Nata looks lovely."

Papa chuckled, and his black eyes twinkled. "Yes, Mama, but she is not the only one who looks lovely."

Mama giggled. "Oh, Papa."

It was nice to hear them laugh and tease. Papa always said that Mama was the one elbee that made his life full of laughter, since he could sometimes become serious with the strain of trying to keep everyone healthy. Indeed, Mama had the best sense of humor, and frequently spent time cheering others up. She had left the life of a hunter behind for Papa, but Mama always said that tracking down all of the crazy herbs that Papa needed for healing was just as dangerous as hunting. Considering recent events, Nata would not even begin to contemplate arguing against that fact.

The three of them walked the short distance to the big tree in the center of the colony where they held all of the celebrations. The colony was connected by a series of intricate walkways, interwoven with elban tree branches. Their magical leaves wove spells to hide their colony. The Elbano Colony was named after the trees that kept them safe, but Nata remembered the name of another colony, Elbana, that was rarely mentioned in stories.

I wonder if that is yet another story that has a

basis in fact.

The colony elders, Muga and Pangos, were standing in front of the doors to the Great Hall. When Papa, Mama, and Nata arrived, the elders bowed their heads at Papa before they bowed their heads to Nata as they opened the doors. Nata was rather startled.

Oh! They must have heard about me becoming a sorceress. Master Pukas did say that it would be difficult to keep that under wraps. I just didn't expect it to be that fast.

Inside the Great Hall, three big fireplaces were ablaze. Long tables were set up in a circular fashion around the room. Several of the hunters were present, gathered around the fires cooking. Mama was quick to join them. Soon she was busy trading tales about the hunt. Nobody was foolish enough to let Mama try cooking.

Candles were hung from the rafters giving the room a golden glow. The aroma of food made her stomach rumble. It looked like everyone from the colony was already here.

Nata felt a knot of anxiety in her stomach ease as it seemed that no one else was going to single her out for any special treatment.

I hope they don't make me give a speech or something.

She followed Papa as he wove a path through the crowd. Papa took the big basket of pina fruit

Nata was carrying, and placed it on the table. Mrs. Kimo started talking to Papa about some healing remedies, so Nata wandered off in search of Nole. Nata walked around the room careful to step over baskets, and small children playing on the floor.

"Ah! Nata, why the long face?" beamed Mr. Kimo.

He was wiping the sweat off of his brown leathery face with a red bandana. Nata was just relieved that he was treating her normally.

"Have you seen Nole?"

"He was outside gathering firewood with Juma."

"Thanks Mr. Kimo," she called over her shoulder.

She didn't hear his reply for she was already walking towards the back door. Nata popped through the doorway, and hit Nole with a thump that knocked them both onto the floor.

Firewood flew everywhere.

"Yikes!" Nole exclaimed.

"Oh no!"

"Are you hurt?"

Nata shook her head. "I should be asking you that. Sorry I ran into you."

"Not to worry," he tucked a curly black tendril of hair behind his pointed ear.

"Here, let me help." Nata got up, and started to pick up the firewood.

Nole held out his arms so that she could stack the firewood in them. "Nice hair."

Nata blushed. "Thanks."

Trust Nole to be so nonchalant about it.

"My, my," Juma smiled.

He was shaking his head, as he walked past them, with his own arms full of firewood. Nole looked at her with such a sheepish grin that she had to giggle. Then the gong sounded, a signal that it was time for the speech. Nole and Nata brought the firewood inside, and stacked it against the wall.

It was custom for a speech of gratitude for a safe and successful hunt to be given before the celebration. Everyone was listening to Muga while he gave the speech. His red curly hair glinted in the candlelight, while his arms swept up and down as he spoke. Nole and Nata tiptoed to their seats. She could hear her stomach rumble, and the aroma of food on the table in front of her made her nose twitch. Just when she felt her stomach would make a huge noise, and disrupt the speech, Muga finished. At the end of his speech, he had made a small acknowledgement for her now being a sorceress before he straightened his hunting vest, and bowed.

There was an audible sigh heard around the room, then everyone clapped, and started to eat. Nata eyed the rest of the elbee's around the Great

Hall, but none of them seemed to expect anything of her. She found the last knot of tension in her body dissolve as she set about enjoying the evening.

After the feasting came the stories, music, and dancing. The first songs were about the hunt, and the warriors danced while the rest sang. After the warriors danced, Mimo started singing a silly bird song.

Chirp, chirp, went the bird in the tree,

Why tree, are you down upon your knee?

Why you silly bird can't you see,

I am an elbee not a tree.

Oh! My! Said the bird looking at me,

Chirp, chirp, said the bird let me be,

Can't you see I am sitting in my tree?

Of course, the whole song was a great deal longer, and caused an explosion of laughter. That was the point. Hunting was stressful work. Hunters also had to spend a great deal of time being as quiet as possible to be both safe, and to make sure their prey didn't notice them. Celebrations were the perfect time for hunters to spend their time laughing and relaxing.

"It's time for the Motche," Muga said.

Laughter rang throughout the room.

Nata looked at Nole. "My favorite dance."

"Come on," Nole took her hand.

Mama and Papa sat, and cheered the dancers. Usually, Mama and Papa would join in, but she had overhead Papa telling Mama she should give it some more time to recover. Nata and Nole danced side by side until the Motche ended.

Red faced and winded from the vigorous, twisting dance, Nole pulled her over to a quiet corner near Mama and Papa.

"Nole, do I seem like the same person to you?"

"Of course, what's wrong?"

"I don't know."

"Nata..., is there something more to this sorceress situation than learning to use magic to heal?"

"Yes..., but Master Pukas hasn't told me what yet."

Nole blinked his blue eyes. "Why?"

"Some things he wanted me to keep secret, and he said he is trying not to overwhelm me."

Nole waved his hand in the air. "That's okay, when you find out, and can tell me, I'll help you figure out what you want to do."

"Thanks Nole."

"That's what friends are for."

Thank goodness I have always been able to count on Nole. I wish his parents had survived that hunt years ago. It's a shame he never knew them.

Years ago there had been a shortage of food. The initial hunt had brought less food than they needed, so the hunters had to go out scavenging for food in the winter. It was dangerous work, and Nole's parents had been some of the best hunters. Mama had been good friends with Nole's parents from her days as a hunter herself, and Papa had become friends with them as a result.

Nole's papa had been killed in the cold of that winter hunt. His mama had been gravely injured in the same fight, but managed to get to Mooto in order to fly back to the colony. His mama's injuries were too severe even for her papa, and she died not to long after making it back.

Mama and Papa both felt some responsibility towards young Nole at the time as the child of their good friends, so more often than not Nole spent a lot of time with them. Nole lived with one of the other hunters though. It made sense as that was what he wanted to grow up to be.

Nata sighed as they listened to the last of the story Ninga was reciting:

> *Tinka smiled at Nimo. "Happy hunting, I will wait for you."*
>
> *Nimo smiled. "I will dream about you, my love."*
>
> *On the back of Reeka, Nimo flew off into the sunrise.*

After the story, the dancing continued. The colony would spend the night celebrating that way, dancing, singing, and listening to stories until the next morning when the suns started to rise. Having seen the beauty of a moonlit night, Nata wished they could have these celebrations under the light of the moons. Maybe someday that would be possible, but for now she was going to enjoy celebration. One thing that puzzled her was Papa leaving partway through the evening.

Hmm..., I wonder what he's up too?

—Chapter 15—

While eating a late lunch the afternoon after the celebration of the successful hunt, she pondered the strange expression on Mama's face. She was being very mysterious as she took out Nata's ceremonial clothes and beads from the big chest. Mama herself was already dressed in her ceremonial clothes.

What's going on? I didn't know there were any ceremonies planned soon, let alone today.

Nata heard the sound of dragon's feet walking in Meeka's lair, and Papa talking. She felt excited, yet she wasn't quite sure why.

"Come here please Nata. Let's get you ready."

Nata chewed her lip. "Did I miss the notice about a ceremony?"

Mama gave Nata a hug, and kissed her forehead. "No, don't feel too bad Nata. I just found out about this ceremony this morning myself. I'm glad that I am well enough to attend it. Come on now."

The first thing that Mama did was help her put on her ceremonial dress. Her dress was a dark purple, and had beaded lavender elban leaves sewn all over the dress. Nata swiped the corn muffin that was the last of her lunch to eat before Mama took her time weaving the beads into Nata's hair. Papa walked into the room just as Mama was finishing up, and Nata was reaching for her earrings.

"Well, well, what have we here?" Papa winked. "I'm just in time for the finishing touch it seems."

Without further ado, he handed Nata a small package wrapped in purple elban leaves. The elbees of the colony gathered fallen elban leaves for many purposes including clothing dyes and packaging materials. It was fortunate that the forest animals ate up the elban leaves that fell, otherwise they would end up buried in leaves.

Nata opened the package and gasped. Inside, there were a brand new set of ceremonial earrings. The tiny beads were stitched together in the design of the elban trees with dark purple leaves and light lavender branches.

"Oh Papa," Nata breathed. "They're beautiful!"

Papa beamed. "I snuck away last night to make them. Here let me help you put them on."

"Thank you Papa." Nata whispered.

Nata had to blink tears out of her eyes as Papa put the earrings in her ears, and kissed her forehead.

Mama laughed. "I think you did a splendid job dear."

He smiled at Mama, and kissed her forehead too. "All ready to go?"

Nata swallowed the last bite of her savored corn muffin, and gave Papa a puzzled look. "Go where?"

I've never heard of a ceremony being held outside of the colony.

Papa almost seemed to be bouncing in excitement. "Just you wait and see."

Nata blinked at Papa in confusion.

Mama huffed. "Ignore him dear. He's had too many corn muffins this afternoon."

Papa pouted, and Nata giggled as they headed into Meeka's lair. She was quite surprised, both Meeka and Mooto were there. Where Mooto was, her friend Nole was usually to be found, but she saw neither tail nor fur of her friend as she looked around. Papa must have guessed who she was looking for, because he shook his head.

Hmmm, so Nole won't be coming today.

Papa nodded towards Meeka. "You and Mama will ride on Meeka today, while I ride Mooto."

"What's going on?" Nata asked.

Meeka piped up. "I made a petition. Master Pukas will explain further when we get where we are going, but for your part all you need to do is follow your heart, listen to your magic, and answer as you feel appropriate. There are none in judgement of you this day."

But there is going to be a judgement of Meeka then? I don't understand what is going on at all.

She noticed the purple locks of hair between Meeka's forehead and neck were beaded and braided in the ceremonial style as well. Mooto kept his hair short out of grief over his inability to protect Nole's parents. She and Nole had talked about it, and they both hoped that one day Mooto would feel he could grow it out again. What hair he did have wasn't long enough to bead or braid, but his red scales glistened in the morning sunlight.

Quite curious about what was going on, she climbed up behind Mama on Meeka's back as they left the colony. The first thing she noticed was that they were flying east instead of north. She watched their shadows glide over the water as they flew over their swimming hole. Nata's curiosity increased as they kept flying east. She glanced down at the forest beneath them, like a dark green lake. The trees grew so close together, it was impossible to see the ground. Finally, the forest ended, and the land below became rolling grassy hills.

Her excitement grew the closer they got to the mountains. They flew between two mountain peaks topped with white snow, their grey slopes bare of trees. The cool air made her skin tingle. Something huge and dark loomed ahead of them.

Nata gasped. "It's Drakonare."

Drakonare was shrouded in a white mist, which seemed to draw back as they flew into it. They flew past blackened elban trees to a huge tree, the heart of Drakonare.

Dragon's Spire, the father of the elban trees that shield our colony, created from magic.

Its bark charred black. The branches bare of its chameleon leaves. When they got closer, she saw two black sand dragons standing on either side of the entrance. Meeka and Mooto landed on a ledge where a tunnel of blackened twisted branches led inside the tree.

Wow!

The two dragons bowed their heads at them. Meeka, Mooto, Mama, and Papa bowed in return. Nata was so taken by surprise that she forgot to bow as she stared at them. The dragons faced forward again to become silent sentinels. Papa climbed off of Mooto's back, and came to stand beside Meeka while she and Mama climbed down. Mama took one of

Nata's hands, while Papa took the other. They walked inside the tunnel entrance with Meeka close behind them, and Mooto bringing up the rear.

The wide tunnel grew darker as they advanced. At the end of the tunnel, they stepped out into a large chamber lit by a small fire in the center. Charred branches lay crushed and broken on the floor. Nata could hear the crunch of lifeless leaves as their group progressed forward into the room.

She glanced around as they walked towards the center. It seemed to be filled with a sea of dragons. The firelight glimmered off the rainbow of colored scales to dazzle her eyes. Their eyes seemed to gleam as they watched them. Excitement throbbed in the air, and she felt a knot in her stomach.

They stopped in front of Dree, the leader of the sand dragons of their colony, and everyone bowed. This time Nata was just grateful that she remembered to bow too.

I wonder how Dree managed to fly so far?

Nata was startled when Master Pukas appeared beside Papa. Slowly the dragons formed a circle around them. Mooto moved away from their group to stand in the circle near Dree.

"Let the petition begin," Dree bellowed.

She looked up at Papa, he smiled, and patted her shoulder.

Mama wrapped her in a hug. "Just be yourself. I love you, and we are both so proud of you."

Mama and Papa stepped forward, bowed to Dree, and walked over to stand beside Mooto.

"Master Pukas," Nata whispered. "What is going on?"

"Ah," he whispered back, "there is another aspect to being a sorcerer or sorceress, which is a bond with a dragon for protection, and provide an anchor for your magic. Considering how badly waiting to awakening your magic affected you, and the way you healed Meeka without being fully awakened gave us the knowledge of who your bonded had a potential to be, we thought it best to make sure this bond happened as quickly as possible just in case."

"Oh, okay... It's not going to hurt, or put me to sleep is it?"

Master Pukas snorted. "It shouldn't do either, but one never knows. I never had the opportunity to learn the official way this ceremony is supposed to go, so my sister and I have been consulting with the dragons to find the closest approximation we can."

Master Pukas smiled faintly at her before he stepped forward, bowed before Dree, then stood beside him.

Dree looked at Meeka and then Nata. *"Today I stand for Spree, Master Pukas's bonded dragon, as he has so graciously joined Mistress Megg and her bonded dragon protecting the skies for our gathering this day. Bear witness, one of our number has petitioned to be the bonded of this young sorceress. For it is the sacred duty of dragon kind to protect the magic users that nurture our world. Meeka, what proof do you offer that you should be this sorceress's bonded?"*

Meeka bowed. *"Honored elder, I bear the tale of our recent journeys as proof of my capability for her defense, my willingness to go wither the magic leads her, and my compatibility as witnessed by Master Pukas. The hunt for the ammera flower for use in healing, the defense of her person against the sand worm when she found her catalyst, our battle against the mere crawler, my subsequent healing, carrying her where she needed to go, and hiding when fighting was untenable."*

Dree nodded. *"Yet, for all your adventures, you were not able to fully protect her. Would you still petition this bond?"*

Meeka lashed her tail. *"I would."*

Master Pukas turned to Nata. *"And you, young sorceress, would you accept Meeka as your bonded that she shall be your trusted companion and protector even knowing of her failure to completely protect you? You are free to refuse, accept, or choose another from among those present should you feel they would suit you better. But remember a bond with a dragon will last until death, so take you time in answering."*

Nata took a deep breath, and closed her eyes.

This was a big decision that would affect the rest of her life, but at the same time it was no decision at all. She had grown up with Meeka. She was family to her, and many of her fondest memories had her present. There was no other dragon that she could see as her bonded, but just to be sure she tried to listen for her magic.

She had no idea what she was looking for, but as she listened she heard the melody again. Not loud and unbearable, but soft and content. As she listened she thought of Meeka and what the future might hold for them together. The melody seemed to dance with joy.

Nata opened her eyes. *"Honored Elder, I would. She has been a kind and loyal friend. I could ask no more of any other than what she has already proved willing to give."*

"So be it," Dree intoned.

Master Pukas's eyes sparkled. *"Nata, to complete this bond place your hands upon Meeka snout, listen to your magic, and speak the words 'Na dora nana dragnano'."*

Nata turned towards Meeka, who had lowered her head to make it easier for her to reach. As she looked into Meeka's eyes she saw all the fierce protectiveness, and fond affection of a sister. Nata smiled as she closed her eyes, and reached again for that melody deep inside. She heard it faster this time though now it seemed ripe with anticipation in it song. Reaching out, she heard another melody. In fact, there were several, but none so close or familiar as the one that sang beneath her fingertips.

She let her melody and Meeka's blend into a smooth harmony before she spoke the words. Nay, they sounded as if she had sung them in tune with their magic. *"Na dora nana dragnano."*

With her eyes closed, Nata did not see the purple light that wrapped around her first before it enveloped Meeka. Nor did she see how an invisible wind whipped through their hair as if they were speeding through the sky. For those present, they could hear the echo of the harmony as Nata spoke the words. The light intensified until it was almost blinding before it fell away leaving Meeka with several white highlights running throughout her purple hair.

Nata opened her eyes, and tried to blink away the tears. There might have been more said, but she was too busy basking in the harmony of their new bond to hear. Little did Nata know how much she was going to need Meeka in the near future.

About the Authors

Lucy and Lizzy Grimm are the writers of Grimm's Imaginarium. They believe that imagination has no limits, and thus have taken to writing stories from their imaginations. The mother and daughter team enjoy writing supportive family stories dosed with various levels of humor. Bringing joy and laughter to their readers is a grand bonus in their eyes. So grab a comfortable spot, maybe grab some family too, and get ready to be transported along with the authors to whatever realm of fiction these two decide to visit.

If you enjoyed the book, keep up-to-date with future titles by visiting or subscribing to: https://grimmsimaginarium.com.

A tale of tails from the Authors:

While writing this story we discovered that the bag turned into a satchel, at times it was a pack, and, not to be forgotten, the pouch. This occurred often to our ever-growing amusement. We decided to end this dilemma by settling on Nata carrying a pouch. We believe this made Nata very happy. Lizzy, as always it has been a pleasure to write this story with you.

Made in the USA
Monee, IL
09 June 2023

35362080R00089